KiD POWER

**Other APPLE® PAPERBACKS
You Will Want to Read:**

The Cybil War
  by Betsy Byars

Dreams of Victory
  by Ellen Conford

The Girl With the Silver Eyes
  by Willo Davis Roberts

Nothing's Fair in Fifth Grade
  by Barthe DeClements

The Pinballs
  by Betsy Byars

With a Wave of the Wand
  by Mark Jonathan Harris

Yours Till Niagara Falls, Abby
  by Jane O'Connor

KiD POWER

by
Susan Beth Pfeffer

Illustrated by
Leigh Grant

AN
APPLE
PAPERBACK

SCHOLASTIC INC.
New York Toronto London Auckland Sydney

ISBN 0-590-42607-9

24   0/0

Printed in the U.S.A.   40

For Joyce Wadler,
who kept me going.

Chapter One

This is about how I found my true calling.

According to my father, I found it pretty young in life. (I'm eleven going on twelve.) He didn't find his until he was in college. He's a lawyer for labor unions, and he doesn't like my true calling at all. If he'd had any say about it, I might never have found it.

I guess my mother's most responsible for it. Mom found her true calling when she was in college, too. She majored in sociology and got her degree, but then she married Dad and had my sister Carol and me. When I was eight, and Carol ten, she went back to school and got her master's degree. Last year she got a job as a social worker in the city. She really enjoyed the work, and I didn't mind not having her home too much. Things were going pretty well until this summer, when Mom got laid off.

"Municipal cutbacks," she told us one evening after supper. It was the very end of June. Carol and I had been out of school for less than a week, and we'd both been looking forward to summer at home. I hate camp, and Carol said she'd outgrown it. Besides, she'd just gotten a job delivering newspapers. She'd been waiting for the job for months, and when there was finally an opening, she wasn't about to give it up for a summer of archery and leathercrafts.

"We've known for a couple of weeks," Dad said. "We were hoping there might be some last minute rescuing of the program, but now it's too late."

"Today was my last day," Mom said with a sigh. She looked really depressed about it.

"What're you going to do now?" Carol asked. Carol is very practical.

"I'm going to look for another job," Mom said. "I don't know how much luck I'll have, but I'll give it a try."

"You'll find something," I said.

"Thanks, Janie," Mom said and smiled at me.

"In the meantime you can get unemployment insurance," Carol said.

"What a cheerful thought," Mom said. "Well, I guess it'll keep the wolf from the door."

"There isn't going to be any wolf," Dad said. Dad's family didn't have much money when he was a kid, and he's a little sensitive about jokes like that. "It was nice having your mother's salary coming in, but we can do just fine without it. After all, we did up until last year."

"So we'll keep going just the way we have been?" Carol asked.

"Absolutely," Dad said.

"And Janie and I'll get those ten-speed bikes you promised us?" she continued. Carol can be positively ruthless at times.

"Of course," Mom said.

"Now wait a second, Meg," Dad said to Mom. "We're not going to starve, but I think we should be careful before we spend our money on luxuries."

"My bike is not a luxury," Carol said. "I need it for my paper route."

"And what about the bike you already have?" Dad asked.

"I've outgrown it," Carol said.

"Maybe we should get Carol a new bike, and give Janie Carol's old one," Mom suggested.

"Mom!" I shouted. "You promised me a new one, too."

"But that was when I had my job," she said. "Oh, I don't know."

"You'll just have to make do," Dad said. When he gets that tone in his voice, firm and no-nonsensy, I usually give up. Not Carol, though.

"I have an idea," she said. "If you have the money for one new bike, why don't you give half of it to me, and half of it to Janie. Then we'll each come up with the other half, and we'll both get new bikes without it costing you so much."

"Matching funds," Mom said. "That's a very clever idea, Carol. What do you think, Art?"

"Where do the girls think they'll come up with their ends?" Dad asked. "Apply to the Ford Foundation for grants?"

"I already have my half," Carol said. "Or pretty close to it." She smiled triumphantly.

"That's not fair," I said. "Then Carol gets her bike and I don't."

"It's not my fault I save my money," Carol said and sneered at me. Carol always saves her money, and I always spend mine. That's a sore point between us. When I buy comic books, she reads them, and then she doesn't buy any of her own. She used to play with my paper dolls too, and I'd catch her coloring in my coloring books all the time. That way she didn't have to spend a cent of her allowance and she put it in her savings account. Last year she started babysitting, and now with the paper route too, she'd been able to save up lots of money, while I kept spending mine on comic books. And now all that thrift was about to pay off for her. She always said it would.

"It's not fair to prevent Carol from getting her bike just because Janie doesn't know the value of a dollar," Dad said. Dad really admires thrift in people. "I think we should see about splitting expenses on a bike with Carol, and then if Janie ever manages to save up her allowance, we can do the same for her. In the meantime, she can use Carol's old bike."

"That sounds fair to me too," Mom said. You could see that, as far as they were concerned, the conversation was ended.

When you're the youngest in the family, you get used to having conversations ended by everybody else even though you haven't finished. But this time I wasn't about to put up with it.

"Wait just one second," I said, trying to sound less like a kid and more like an injured party. Mom and

Dad both have a lot of sympathy for injured parties. "I'd have to save my allowance for a whole year to raise that kind of money. Maybe even longer."

"Longer," Carol said, computing my allowance and the cost of ten-speed bikes.

"A whole year without anything," I said. "No comic books, no bubble gum . . ."

"How heartbreaking," Dad said.

"No pens," I said. "No pencils. No sketch pads. No intellectual reading matter. Nothing for a solid year. I'll die of culture shock."

"That is asking a lot of her," Mom said. Mom likes the idea that I draw. I'm not very good, but I enjoy doing it, and she keeps hoping.

"No birthday presents for anybody else," I said, looking mournfully at Carol. I make a point of getting her really good presents every year. That way she's pretty nice to me for about a month before her birthday and a week after.

"I'll have a regular deprived childhood," I concluded. "Just the kind I thought Dad didn't want me to have."

I overshot my mark there a little. Dad got angry-looking and said, "I didn't know the lack of bubble gum constituted a deprived childhood."

"Janie's overstating it," Mom said. "But she has a point. The only way we can do matching funds is if she can earn some money for herself, the way Carol's been doing. That's how Carol can afford to do it, after all."

My parents don't seem to realize that Carol hasn't spent a penny voluntarily since birth. That's why when

I used to complain about her using my coloring books and paper dolls and comic books, I never got any sympathy. "Carol lets you share her things," Mom always said, not understanding that Carol didn't have anything to share. On our parents' birthdays, she gives them something she made, a picture she drew (with my paper and pencils, usually), or some clay thing she made during art class in school, and Mom and Dad always seem to appreciate it even more because she made it. She gives me presents that she was given for her birthday the year before and never used. Carol carries stinginess to unheard-of heights.

I realized then that Carol must really want the bike a lot if she was willing to put up some of her money for it. I wondered if that might give me some room to negotiate.

"Maybe I could take over Carol's paper route," I said thoughtfully. "That way I could earn the money really fast."

"You cannot," Carol said. "That's my route. I waited for months for that opening, and I'm not about to give it up to you just because you can't save anything."

Next year I'd give her a handmade gift for her birthday, I decided. Let's see how she liked that.

"There are lots of jobs Janie could do besides a paper route," Mom said. "And she does have the whole summer to earn some money."

"What kind of jobs?" I asked. "Do you think I could babysit?"

"Maybe," Mom said.

"Hey, that's not fair," Carol said. "You wouldn't let

me babysit until this year. You said I was too young."

"Janie is too young," Dad said. "She's too young for any kind of work."

"I am not," I said. "There are lots of things I could do."

"Sure," Carol said. "Name one."

I couldn't. I knew there had to be things I could do, but I couldn't think of a single thing. "I help out here a lot," I said lamely.

"Considerably more than Carol does," Mom said. "Janie is a very good worker and a very responsible girl. All she has to do is let people in the neighborhood know that she's available for odd jobs, and I bet she'll get plenty of work."

"What kind of odd jobs?" Dad said. "I don't think Janie should go around asking for handouts of any kind."

"This wouldn't be a handout," Mom said and sighed. "Honestly, Art, I know you grew up in the city and all that, but believe me, there's nothing wrong with Janie helping people weed their gardens, and things like that. She can run errands for Mrs. Edwards down the block, for instance. That poor woman finds it so hard to get around these days. She'd love it if somebody came over every day and asked her if there was something from the shops she wanted."

"That's a good idea," I said. I liked Mrs. Edwards; she was a nice old lady. "Do you think Grandma might have something I could do?"

"I wouldn't be surprised," Mom said. "As a matter of fact she was talking to me just the other day about cleaning out her attic. Janie could help her move the stuff and throw some of it out. Actually, I'd prefer if Janie did help. I don't like the idea of Mom all alone in that attic too long during the summer. It gets awfully hot in there."

"I'll advertise," I said. "I bet before too long I'll have thousands of jobs to do."

"Advertise?" Dad said. "What do you want, commercials on television, or will full-page magazine ads do?"

"I'll put a sign up in the grocery store," I said. "That's all I meant."

"I'm still not sure I like the idea," Dad said.

"I think we should let Janie give it a try," Mom said. "It's always possible nothing will come of it."

"I'll get lots of jobs," I said.

"I certainly hope so," Mom said. "Now if that topic's exhausted, I'd like to check out the newspaper want ads for jobs for myself."

Carol and I both got up. I had the feeling Dad wanted to talk to Mom some more about it, but I was pretty sure Mom would convince him. Mom can be very convincing when she wants to be.

I followed Carol upstairs, then went to my room and got my sketch paper and magic markers. I walked to her room and knocked on her door.

"Go away," Carol said.

"I've got to talk to you," I said and went in anyway. Carol always tells me to go away, but I usually don't pay any attention to her.

"What do you want?" Carol asked. I could see she was checking out her savings account book to see how much money she had.

"I was wondering if you'd do the lettering for my sign?" I asked. "You're such a good letterer."

"Okay," Carol said, putting the book down. "I guess I'd better cooperate or I might not get my bike. But you can't have my paper route."

"That was a dumb idea on my part," I agreed. "Thanks, Carol."

"Sure," she said, and took the paper and markers. "You really think you'll save any of the money you'll earn? I bet you spend it as soon as you get it."

"I will not," I said. "I'll save it all until I have enough money for my half of the bike."

"Good luck," she said. "Now what do you want this sign to say?"

"I don't know," I said. "I guess it should have my name and phone number on it, so people'll know who to call."

"It's going to need more than that," Carol said. "You're going to have to say what you do, or else nobody'll call."

"But I don't know yet what I do," I said. "I'll do whatever people hire me to do."

"Then you need some sort of all-purpose name," she said. "Something catchy that people'll notice."

"Like the AFL-CIO," I said.

"That wasn't quite what I had in mind," Carol said. "You need a name like the stuff they sell in stores."

"I refuse to be called Fab or Tide or Swanson's TV Dinners," I said.

"All right, we'll wait on that," Carol said. "You need a slogan, too."

"I figured one out already," I said. " 'No job too big or small.' "

"That's not bad," Carol said, "Especially the small part."

"Carol!"

"I'm serious," she said. "You should let everybody know you're just a kid. People pay kids less. It's called child labor, and you don't have to give them minimum wage. That's one reason Dad didn't like the idea."

"What should I charge then?" I asked.

"A dollar an hour," Carol said. "Unless they want you to do something really hard. And your name should have something about being a kid in it."

"Kid Power," I said. "No job too big or small."

"Perfect," Carol said. "Kid Power it is."

And that's how it all started.

Chapter Two

First thing next morning, I put my Kid Power sign up on the supermarket bulletin board. I knew people looked there a lot, and I was sure plenty of people from the development where we live would notice it. I went home and called Grandma next. She said she'd be delighted to have some help with the attic, so I took the bus to the outskirts of town, and then walked the rest of the way to her house.

I helped her for three hours, carrying boxes out of the attic and helping her decide what to keep and what to throw out. It seemed almost criminal to ask for money, especially since she gave me lemonade and cookies, and showed me Mom's baby pictures. We spent more time just talking than actually cleaning, and I carried practically as much back to the attic as I'd taken out, but Grandma claimed we'd done a lot of good work that day, and insisted on paying me my $3. I offered her a special family rate, but she said she wouldn't hear of it.

She also said if she heard of anybody who needed help with odd jobs she'd recommend me. I had one last cookie, kissed her good-bye, and walked back to the bus. I didn't get home until pretty late in the afternoon, and when I did, I found Mom sitting in the kitchen, circling job ads in the paper.

"There you are," she said. "You got a phone call."

"Who?" I asked. "Lisa?" Lisa's my best friend, and she calls me all the time.

"No, a call for Kid Power," Mom said. "I took the woman's name and number down and said you'd call her back just as soon as you got in."

"Where is it!" I shouted. Somehow a job from your grandmother doesn't count the way a job from a stranger does.

"Calm down," Mom said. "Right here." She handed me a scrap of paper with "Mrs. Dale, 342-4456" written on it.

I called the number, and took a deep breath. That's a trick my father taught me. It makes your voice sound deeper and it relaxes you.

"Hello?"

"Hello, Mrs. Dale?"

"Speaking."

"This is Janie Golden of Kid Power calling."

"Oh yes," Mrs. Dale said. "I saw your poster in the supermarket today, and I was wondering if you could help me."

"I'm sure I can," I said, trying to sound adult and authoritative.

"I'm having a yard sale on Saturday," she said. "And

your sign made me think it would be a good idea if I had someone at the sale just to look after the kids people bring with them. The little ones are always getting their hands on things, and without meaning to—well, sometimes they take things home with them."

"So you'd want me to look after them," I said. "Kind of day-care."

"Exactly," Mrs. Dale said. "Do you think you could fit me into your schedule?"

"I'm sure I could," I said, pretending to look at a calendar. "Yes, I'm free on Saturday. What time would you want me there?"

"The sale is scheduled to start at ten," she said, "which means the first customers will be there by eight-thirty. It's supposed to end at four, so that would be a full day's work for you."

"No problem," I said. "I'll be there at eight-thirty."

"What do you charge?" she asked.

I breathed deep again. "A dollar an hour," I said.

"Oh, that's quite reasonable," Mrs. Dale said. "I'm sure if someone is there to watch after the children, their parents will be more likely to buy things."

"There is one more thing," I said.

"Certainly," Mrs. Dale said. "What is it?"

"Kid Power is just getting started, and I could use some free publicity," I said. "Would you mind if I put up a little sign, like I have at the supermarket, at your yard sale?"

"Of course not," Mrs. Dale said. "I like an enterprising young woman. I'll see you Saturday then—120 Woodhaven Road."

"Saturday," I said, writing down the address. "Thank you Mrs. Dale."

"Thank you, Janie," she said, and we hung up.

"I got a job!" I hollered, running over to hug Mom. "Eight-thirty to four. At a dollar an hour, that's $7.50. And I earned $3.00 at Grandma's. I'm going to be rich!"

"It might rain on Saturday," Mom said. "Don't spend your money before you see it."

"I'm not going to spend any of it," I said. "I'm going to save it all just like Carol until I'm the richest person in junior high."

"Don't invest in municipal bonds then," Mom said glumly, looking at the paper.

"Are there any jobs you could do?" I asked.

"Not that I can see," she said. "I'm either underqualified or overqualified or just plain not qualified. There doesn't seem to be much for an unemployed social worker these days."

"You'll find something," I said.

"I sure hope so," she said. "So tell me. How's Grandma?"

We talked until Dad came home and then I told him all about the money I'd earned and the money I was going to earn. "I'm still not sure this is such a good idea," he grumbled over supper, but I ignored him. I could tell from the three dollars in my wallet that this was one fine idea.

The next day I decided to drum up some business. I walked over to Mrs. Edwards' house and rang her bell. I could hear her coming to the door and waited until she did. Mrs. Edwards has arthritis and doesn't walk too fast.

"Why Janie, what a pleasant surprise," she said. "Come in, honey."

"Thank you," I said, feeling a little guilty. It didn't seem right to be asking Mrs. Edwards for a job when she was just so happy to have some company. "How're you feeling?" I asked.

"About the same," she said. "And how are you?"

"I'm fine," I said. "My mom got laid off though."

"Isn't that terrible," she said. "I was wondering if all those cutbacks would affect her."

"They did," I said. "And until she gets a new job, I've decided to earn some money on my own. You see, Carol and I were supposed to get new bikes, and now we can't afford to, so I'm trying to earn money for mine."

"Isn't that fine of you," Mrs. Edwards said. "Tell me Janie, what kind of work do you think you'll get?"

"Well I've already gotten some jobs," I said. "You see I'm calling myself Kid Power. I'm going to run errands for people. On Saturday I'm going to watch the kids at a yard sale."

"I think it's just wonderful that you're helping your family out this way," Mrs. Edwards said. "Is there anything I can do for you?"

"I was thinking about how you can't get out very much anymore," I said. "I was wondering if you'd like me to check in on you every day and see if there's anything you'd like from the drugstore or grocery or library."

"What a good idea," Mrs. Edwards said. "As a matter of fact, I would like having someone to run errands like that for me. It's such a bother to get around, and there are times I feel so isolated. How much do you charge?"

"Fifty cents," I said, giving Mrs. Edwards my newly created senior citizen discount rate. If I'd known about it the day before, I would have given it to Grandma.

"Monday through Friday," Mrs. Edwards said. "I usually have someone over during the weekends to keep me company."

"Great," I said. "Thank you Mrs. Edwards. Is there anything I can do for you today?"

"If you could return my library books, I'd really appreciate it," she said. "They're a couple of days overdue, and I'm so embarrassed about it. But now I'll never have to worry about overdue books again."

"I'll be glad to return them," I said. "Do you want me to take any out for you while I'm there?"

"Not today," she said, and gave me a dollar bill. "Keep the change."

"But the overdue fines won't be very much," I said as she handed the books to me. There were only two of them.

"I'm sure you'll earn it by summer's end," Mrs. Edwards said. "Besides, I like to reward such initiative and family spirit. Now run along, and I'll see you tomorrow morning."

"Thanks a lot, Mrs. Edwards," I said, and left, taking the books and the money with me. I went straight to the library and returned the books. Fifty cents a day would be $2.50 a week. That was $10.00 a month, maybe a little more. Added to the $3.00 I'd already earned, and the $7.50 I was going to earn on Saturday, that was $20.50 for just this month. And I was bound to get other jobs as well. If I earned just $1.00 a day extra for every day in the month, that would be another $31.00, which

would put me at $51.50 for July. And if I made the same in August, I'd make over $100.00 in the summer, which would be more than enough for my bike. I was starting to understand why Carol never spent any of her money. It was more fun just running the figures through my mind and figuring out how much I'd be worth than buying a new comic book would be. Maybe I wouldn't even get the bike. Maybe I'd just save and save until I had a huge amount of money saved, and then I'd do something spectacular with it. I couldn't figure out just what I wanted all that much, but I was sure there would be something by the time I had the money saved.

While I was at the library, I took out *A Child's First Book of Investments*. It looked awfully dull, but I figured it wouldn't hurt to learn about tax shelters. I ran home and found there was nobody there. There was a note from Mom though saying "Carol's out swimming. I'm checking out a possible job. Keep your fingers crossed."

I was kind of annoyed, even though I knew that was unreasonable of me. Suppose somebody had called with a job for me and there was nobody around to take the message? They might never call again, and then I'd be out the money.

I spent the rest of the day waiting for the phone to ring, which it never did, and reading *A Child's First Book of Investments,* which was even duller than it had looked at the library. When Mom came in, I ran downstairs, and asked her how the job interview had gone.

"Don't ask," she growled.

I thought of telling her about Mrs. Edwards right then to cheer her up, but I decided to let it wait until supper time, when I could cheer Dad up with it, too. I helped Mom make supper and set the table for her. Carol had called saying she'd been invited to have supper at her best friend's, so we made a big salad for the three of us. Carol doesn't like salad as much as we do.

"I got another job today," I said, while we were serving ourselves. "I went over to Mrs. Edwards like Mom suggested, and for fifty cents a day, I'm going to run errands for her. That's my senior citizen rate."

"That's very nice," Mom said. She didn't sound too cheered up.

"Mrs. Edwards even gave me some extra money today," I said. "She said she was very impressed with my initiative and family spirit."

"What does family spirit have to do with anything?" Dad asked.

"I told her about Mom getting laid off," I said. "I guess she meant that."

"You told her what?" Dad asked.

"About how Mom got laid off and how you couldn't afford my bike anymore," I said, and bit noisily into a piece of celery.

"Great," Dad said, disgusted. He put his fork down. "Now the whole town's going to think we're some kind of charity case."

"Now Art, don't overstate it," Mom said.

"I'm not overstating it," he said loudly. "Next thing you know Janie'll dress up in rags and beg for contributions for her poor, needy family. Janie, when will you ever learn to keep your mouth shut?"

"I just told Mrs. Edwards the truth," I said. "I didn't think we were keeping it a secret."

"We're not," Mom said. "It's just—well Dad thinks you might have made it sound like we need the money, and that's why you're doing these little jobs."

"Well, isn't that why I am working?" I asked. "Because you can't afford bikes for Carol and me anymore?"

"I can't see why you need new bikes anyway," Dad said. "But if it's going to stop the neighborhood from wondering about my imminent bankruptcy, I'll go out tomorrow and buy you and Carol the most expensive bikes this town has ever seen. Two for each of you, if that'll do it."

It was a good thing Carol wasn't there. That was just the kind of offer she wouldn't have turned down.

"Dad, I'm sorry if I said something wrong," I said. "But please don't make me stop Kid Power. I'm enjoying doing it. I like earning my own money."

"Oh well," Dad said. "I suppose you'll tire of it after a day or so, and then this whole discussion will be moot."

"I will not tire of it," I said, but then I could see Mom shake her head warningly at me, so I kept quiet. I'd just taken another bite of celery when the phone rang. "I'll get it," I said, just to keep the peace a little while longer. "Hello," I said, swallowing rapidly.

"Is this Janie Golden?" the voice asked.

"Yes," I said.

"This is Emma Marks," the woman said. "I'm a friend of Mrs. Edwards."

"Oh yes," I said. "Hello."

"Hello," she said. "I was wondering if you could tell me what dress size you wear?"

"Size 12," I said.

"That's just perfect," she said. "I have a little job for you, if you could take it."

"Sure. What?"

"I have a granddaughter who lives in Oregon," she said. "And I just love sewing things for her, but it's not easy since I don't have her around to try things on. I was wondering if you'd be willing to model the clothes for me while I sew them. How tall are you?"

"Five feet," I said.

"Harriet is four-foot-eleven," she said. "This sounds just ideal. Could you come over tomorrow? I have a half-dozen different projects I've been holding back on, and I'd love to get started on them."

"Sure," I said. "What time should I come over?"

"How about after lunch?" she said. "I live at 22 Curry Road."

"I know where that is," I said. "I'll see you at one then."

"Fine," she said. "Thank you, Janie."

"Thank you," I said and hung up. I walked back to the dining room table and said, "I just got another job."

"It certainly sounds like you're going to have a busy summer," Mom said.

"You'll quit in a week," Dad said.

I didn't say anything. I was too busy adding those extra dollars to the ones I already knew about.

Chapter Three

Cleaning the attic with Grandma was a snap, and there was no trick to asking Mrs. Edwards if she wanted me to run any errands for her. Even being fitted by Mrs. Marks for dresses for her granddaughter Harriet (who sounded like a real creep) wasn't too bad. But babysitting for a bunch of kids at a yard sale was my first real challenge, and I hoped I was up to it.

First of all I insisted that Carol letter another sign for me, and she did, for a dollar. I wasn't too thrilled about paying her at all, but she pointed out if I wanted to be paid for my labor, so did she. It almost hurt to hand that dollar over to her. I hadn't spent a penny that I'd earned since I'd started Kid Power. I'd even bought a little notebook (from my allowance) and started to keep records of who'd paid me what and when. Mom offered to teach me double entry bookkeeping, but I decided to stick to my own system, which recorded all the money coming in and didn't allow for the possibility that any of it might be going out. Except, of course, Carol's dollar.

"You're going to have to spend more money than that," Carol told me a couple of nights before the yard sale.

"Why?" I asked. "You haven't spent any money in ten years."

"But I'm not in business for myself," she said. "People who are in business for themselves always have to spend money. It has to do with gross and net."

"Gross and what?" I asked.

"Gross and net," she said. "That means you have to spend money to make money."

"That doesn't make any sense at all," I said, and walked over to where Dad was reading a book. I knew he wasn't the best choice of people to ask about my business, but Mom was making her daily check of jobs in the paper, and that wasn't to be interrupted. "Dad, can I ask you a question?"

"Sure, honey," he said and put his book down. "You know you can always ask me whatever you want to know."

"What's gross and net?" I asked.

"Gross and what?" he asked.

"Gross and net," I said. "Carol says it has to do with business."

"Oh, that gross and net," he said with a sigh. "You know in some families daughters ask their fathers about how to get boys or improve their fastballs."

"I don't want to get any boys," I said. "And my fastball's just fine. What's gross and net?"

"This conversation is pretty gross, if you ask me," he said.

"Daddy!" I said. "Whatever happened to 'Ask me anything you want?' "

"You're right," he said. "Okay, gross and net are business terms. Let's take that job you did for Grandma. How much did she pay you?"

"Three dollars," I said.

"Okay, your gross profit was three dollars. But it cost you fifty cents to take the bus there and back, right?"

I nodded.

"So if you subtract the fifty cents from the three dollars, you have a net profit of $2.50. The net profit is the gross profit minus expenses."

"And there have to be expenses?"

"Yes, Scrooge," Dad said.

"Then Carol was right," I said.

"That's been known to happen," he said. "Now do you want to learn about profit sharing or capital gains?"

"Not tonight," I said. "Thanks, Dad."

"Come the revolution," he said and grinned. "But if your whole generation is like you, I guess the revolution won't be for a while."

I didn't care about revolutions nearly as much as I did about gross and net. I'd never thought about there being two kinds of profits in the world. I went back to Carol and sat by her feet. Carol likes it when I do that.

"Tell me about spending money to make money," I said.

Carol put down my sign and said, "What do you want to know?"

"How much do I have to spend?"

"That depends," she said. "Now take this yard sale business."

"Yes?"

"If I were in charge of the kids, I'd make sure they had something to keep them busy."

"I've already thought about that," I said. "But if I bring some of my own toys, they might think they're for sale."

"Then bring something else," she said.

"Like what?"

"Like food," she said. "Everybody loves food."

"That's certainly true," I said. "And little kids aren't on diets, so they can eat just about anything."

"Of course, it'll cost you some money," she said. "But it'll make your job easier, and then you'll do it better, and then other people'll be more likely to hire you. That's what I mean by spending money to make money."

"What kind of food do you think I should bring?" I asked. I was hoping she'd suggest something inexpensive.

"I make a really good oatmeal cookie," she said thoughtfully. "It's practically nutritious."

"They are good," I said. "Carol, would you really bake me some?"

"Sure," Carol said.

I got up and hugged her. "Carol, you're the greatest big sister in the whole world!" I shouted. I didn't even care if I disturbed Dad and Mom.

"A dollar a batch," she said coolly.

I broke away from her. "What?"

"You heard me," she said. "A dollar a batch."

"You little cheapskate!" I said.

"Whatever happened to best sister in the world?" Dad asked from his side of the living room.

"Those are my terms," Carol said. "After all, I should be paid too for working in a hot kitchen in July just to bake cookies for some little kids I don't even know."

"You'd be baking them for me," I said.

"That's even worse," she said. "A $1.50 a batch."

"Carol!"

"Okay, a dollar," she said. "How many batches do you want?"

"How many cookies are there to a batch?" I asked.

"A couple of dozen," she said.

I did a little mental arithmetic. "I'll take three batches at fifty cents a batch," I said. "And I won't pay for any burnt cookies, and you have to give me my money back for any cookies I don't sell."

"I will not," she said. "A dollar a batch and you keep what you get."

"Fifty cents and I'll let you make a sign saying you made the cookies," I said. "You might get some business that way."

"A dollar and I get to have the sign anyway," she said.

"I think we need a mediator," I said. "Daddy!"

"You don't have to shout," he said. "Okay, come on over."

Carol and I crossed the room and explained our problem to him. Dad listened and then thought about it.

"How does this sound?" he asked. "Seventy-five cents for each batch, no burnt cookies allowed. That's two dozen unburnt cookies to a batch. Carol gets to advertise, and Janie's responsible for any extra cookies."

"That sounds okay to me," I said. The main thing was

to make sure I didn't have to take any burnt cookies. I wouldn't have put it past Carol to burn them all.

Carol scowled. "I guess it'll be okay," she said. "But I want to make four batches instead of three. It's the same amount of work. All I'd have to do is double the ingredients."

"Are you willing to order another batch?" Dad asked me.

I thought about it. It was better to have too many cookies than too few. But it meant I was going to have a lot of extra cookies, and seventy-five cents less net profit.

"Okay," I said. "But only if Carol throws in two free pitchers of homemade lemonade."

Dad raised his eyebrows, but didn't say anything.

"I get to advertise?" Carol asked.

"Absolutely," I said.

"Deal," she said.

"You'll bake the cookies tomorrow?" I asked.

"I sure will," she said.

"Fine," Dad said. "Now if you'll leave me alone for a while, I'll read my book and think about how many oatmeal cookies this family is going to eat on Sunday."

"None," I said. "I'm going to get rid of each and every one of them if I have to ram them down those kids' throats."

"You'll make a great mother," Dad said and started reading again.

So Carol finished the sign for me, and then she made a sign that said, "Homebaked Oatmeal Cookies by Carol Golden." She decided not to put her phone number down to avoid getting calls from cookie cranks. The next day she made four dozen oatmeal cookies. Mom was out all day going to different employment agencies, so she didn't notice just how much of her ingredients Carol was using.

"These cookies," Carol said to me, as she nibbled on a slightly burnt one, "are pure net profit."

I paid her the three dollars, which lowered Kid Power's net profits considerably. I knew I'd be getting a lot of money the next day, but it still hurt to see so much of the company's profits go into somebody else's hands.

I cleaned the kitchen up for Carol so Mom wouldn't see what a mess she'd made of it. We hadn't discussed who'd do the cleaning, but I figured it was easier to just do it than to negotiate all over again. I packed the cookies into a paper bag, and stuck in a couple of paper plates to put them on. The lemonade she said she'd make after supper.

Mom got in just before Dad did. "How did it go?" I asked while she took her shoes off.

"Nothing," she said, kicking her left shoe clear across the room. "Between all the other social workers that got laid off and all the June college graduates, there are a hundred applications for every job. One of the agencies suggested I get a Ph.D. and teach sociology to future unemployable social workers."

"You'll get a job," I said.

"Sure," she said. "When your father gets in, tell him I'm upstairs taking a nap." She trudged out of the room, leaving her shoes where she'd flung them.

So Dad treated us all to hamburgers and french fries

that night, and we tiptoed around all evening, even though Mom had the airconditioner on and couldn't have heard us anyway. Things were much easier when she had a job. Sure there were some nights when she'd come home tired and depressed from her work, but we never had to tiptoe.

She didn't seem in too bad a mood the next morning when she drove me and the cookies and the lemonade and the signs to Mrs. Dale's house. "I'll pick you up at four," she said, and kissed me on the cheek. "Good luck, honey."

"Thanks, Mom," I said and got out of the car. I could see Mrs. Dale setting out her merchandise on folding tables. There were already people there watching as she unpacked stuff from boxes.

"Hi," I said, walking over to her, holding the pitchers of lemonade carefully. "I'm Janie Golden from Kid Power."

Mrs. Dale smiled at me. "Look at those vultures," she whispered. "Just waiting to swoop down."

"Is there any place I could put my stuff?" I asked. "I brought cookies and lemonade for the kids."

"That's a great idea," she said. "There should be some space at that end of the table. Why don't you put your things there?"

I went to where she pointed and set up. I scotch-taped the two signs to the edge of the table, and put out two platters of cookies. There were still plenty left, so I ate one while I waited for kids to show up.

"Do you think we should put up another sign telling the kids the cookies are for them?" Mrs. Dale asked me as the first customers started going through her stuff.

"I already did," I said and took out another pair of signs. One read, "Kids' Cookies. Free for all kids 12 and under." The other read, "Adult Cookies. 5¢ each."

Mrs. Dale laughed, and handed me a nickel. "I'll have one adult cookie please," she said, and I gave her one from the adult pile. She bit into it and said, "These are very good. You'll probably make more money today than I will."

"I'm just trying to build up my net profit," I said, but before we had more of a chance to talk, some kids came over and started grabbing at the cookies. "Only two per kid," I said.

"Says who?" one of the kids asked.

"Says me," I said.

"The sign doesn't say anything about two cookies a kid," the kid pointed out.

So I took the sign down and changed it to "Kids' Cookies. 2 Free Cookies for all kids 12 and under." The "2" fit in pretty well, but the second "Cookies" was pretty scrunched in.

"As long as the sign says it, I guess it's okay," the kid said and handed me a nickel. "I want one of the adult cookies, too."

"Okay," I said. There was nothing on the sign that said kids couldn't buy the adult cookies if they wanted, so I knew it must be okay.

It was a long, hot, tiring yard sale. The kids stayed away from their parents, and stuck to the cookies and me. The lemonade didn't last the morning, but Mrs. Dale thought that it was such a good idea, she sent me

inside to make some more, which I did. When I came back with a fresh pitcher, I saw a whole family, two grungy-looking parents and three of the dirtiest little kids I've ever seen, steal all but two of the cookies from the adult plate.

I shouted "Hey!" at them, but they just ran away with the cookies. Mrs. Dale came right over though.

"Those awful people," she said. "I knew they were going to steal something before they left. I could tell from the way they were looking around and whispering. I guess we should consider ourselves lucky all they took were the cookies."

"I guess so," I said, and put the lemonade pitcher down.

"Let me pay you for them," she said.

"For the cookies?" I said. "You don't have to do that."

"Of course I should," she said. "A dollar should cover it, don't you think?"

Instead of answering her, I took some of the kid cookies and put them on the adult plate. "They're all the same cookie," I said. "I'm just charging for some of them."

Mrs. Dale laughed. "Janie, you'll be a millionaire before you're twenty-one," she said.

"I thought about charging a quarter for four cookies," I said, "but I decided that was cheating. So I guess I won't get rich that fast."

Mrs. Dale was still laughing when a lady walked over to where I was sitting and asked for an adult cookie. I gave her one and she gave me a nickel.

She ate it very carefully. "This is an excellent oatmeal cookie," she said when she finished. "I'll take a dozen."

"A dozen?" I asked. "I don't sell them by the dozen."

"Why not?" the woman asked.

"I don't know," I said. "It just never occurred to me." I looked through the bag and found a dozen unbroken cookies. There were so few cookies left that I took them out and put them on the plates, and put the lady's dozen cookies back in the bag and handed it to her. She gave me three quarters, and I gave her back her change.

"These cookies remind me of my childhood," she said. "I don't suppose I could get more."

"At sixty cents a dozen?" I asked, doing some quick arithmetic. If I took a ten-cent commission for every dozen cookies, Carol would still be getting fifty cents, which was basically the rate she'd wanted to charge me before I bargained her down. "Sure you can," I said, and gave her my phone number. "That's also the number of Kid Power," I said. "No job too big or small."

"I'll remember that," she said, and started to walk away.

"Don't forget to tell your friends," I called out after her.

"I won't," she called back, and left with her cookies.

Mrs. Dale looked at me and grinned. "You'll make it before you're twenty-one," she said.

I counted the pile of nickels I'd earned already. There was well over two dollars there, and I still had a few cookies left. Even if I didn't sell anymore, and had to give the rest away to the few remaining stragglers, I'd still have cut my business expenses down to less than a dollar and raised my net profit by two.

I smiled back at Mrs. Dale. "I just might at that," I said.

Chapter Four

My best friend, Lisa, couldn't have cared less about gross and net. "Money's money," she said as we sat in my back yard. I'd insisted on staying there just in case the phone rang. Mom was following up on an ad, and Carol was swimming.

"I thought so, too," I said. "But now I know better."

"That's all you care about these days," she said. "Are you going to spend the whole summer working?"

"No, of course not," I said. "I'm not working now, am I?"

"I wouldn't exactly call this playing," she said.

"Okay," I said, getting up. "You want to go someplace, we'll go someplace."

"It's about time," she said and rose. Just as she did, the phone rang.

"Oops," I said, and started running toward the back door. "Well, it might be a job for Mom," I called back to her, but I knew she didn't believe it any more that I did.

I got to the phone by the third ring, and answered it breathlessly. "Hello?"

"Is this Kid Power?" a man asked.

"Yes it is," I said, sounding businesslike. "What can I do for you?"

"Mrs. Edwards suggested I call," the man said. "She said you were available for odd jobs."

"I sure am," I said. "What kind of job do you have in mind?"

"My name is Harry Townsend," he said. "I live two doors away from Mrs. Edwards. The yellow house with the white trim."

"I know," I said. "The one with the beautiful gardens."

"That's the one," he said. "The gardens are my wife's, but she's in the hospital right now for surgery."

"I'm sorry to hear it," I said. I thought it gave my end of the conversation a nice adult sound.

"It's nothing major, but she'll be in the hospital for a little while, and she's concerned that her garden will be overrun with weeds by the time she can start tending it again. Do you know anything about gardening?"

I was no gardening pro, but the summer before, we'd planted a vegetable garden and I could recognize a radish and a tomato with no difficulty at all by September. "I've done some gardening," I said.

"The work wouldn't be very difficult," Mr. Townsend said. "Just simple weeding and fertilizing. Maybe a half hour a day, sometimes a little more. Would you be interested?"

"I charge a minimum of a dollar an hour for each

day's work," I said. "Would you be willing to pay that?"

"Certainly," Mr. Townsend said. "Why don't you come over right now, and I'll tell you what my wife told me while it's still fresh in my mind."

"Sure," I said, and then remembered Lisa. "Uh, a friend of mine is here. Could she come, too?"

"I'd be delighted to have her," he said. "I'll see both of you in a few minutes then."

"Right. And thank you, Mr. Townsend," I said and hung up. I ran back outside and shouted to Lisa, "I got another job!"

"All work and no play," she said, but then she smiled. "What kind of job?"

"Gardening. Come on. We're supposed to go over right now and look at Mrs. Townsend's gardens."

"Mrs. Townsend's?" Lisa asked. "But she has the nicest gardens on the block. Maybe even in town."

"All I'm supposed to do is weed them," I said. "I know the difference between a weed and a flower. Flowers are pretty."

"Janie, you're getting in too deep," Lisa said. "I'd better come with you before you make a complete fool of yourself."

"Just because you're always gardening is no reason to assume other people don't know how to, too," I said, and started for the street.

"Other people may know," Lisa said, running to catch up with me. "Just not you."

But looking at Mrs. Townsend's gardens reassured me. Sure they were beautiful, but they were so neatly laid out, I was sure I'd have no trouble figuring what to keep and what to pull out. Even the bugs sitting on the rose bushes were pretty. They looked like big green ladybugs.

Mr. Townsend was very polite, and showed me where all the gardening tools were. He also gave me a neatly typed list of what Mrs. Townsend wanted done daily, and what she wanted done weekly. I admired her organization. I hoped if I ever had to go into the hospital for surgery, that I'd be that organized with Kid Power.

Lisa, of course, decided to throw her two cents in, by making little comments to Mr. Townsend. He smiled and nodded, but then he said, "Frankly, my wife's the gardener in the family. I hardly know the difference between a weed and a flower."

A man after my own heart. I smiled at him and said "Don't worry, Mr. Townsend. With Kid Power taking care of your garden, you won't have to know the difference."

Lisa walked home with me and offered to help out with the garden, but I didn't pay too much attention to what she was saying. I was more interested in figuring out how much money I was going to earn a week. Five dollars a week from Mr. Townsend, and $2.50 from Mrs. Edwards, and maybe a dollar a week from Mrs. Marks. That was $8.50 guaranteed, except for Mrs. Marks, and I had a feeling I could pretty much count on it. Little Harriet didn't seem to get any clothes except the stuff her grandmother made for her. Plus those jobs, there would be whatever unexpected jobs came up. And all that was pure net, which was the best kind of money there was. "Lisa, I'm going to be rich," I said.

"Money doesn't buy happiness," she said.

"I know that," I said. "But it doesn't buy unhappiness either."

"Want to go to the movies on Saturday?" she asked. "They're having a special matinee of *The Invasion of the Giant Anteaters.*"

"Giant anteaters?" I said. "That sounds pretty good."

"Then you'll come?" she asked. "If you don't go, my mom won't let me go because there's nobody else to go with except my brother, and I absolutely refuse to go with him. He cries at all the scary parts."

Lisa's brother was seven, and they should have made a horror movie about him. "Sure I'll go," I said. "I'll meet you at your house."

"Okay," she said. "But please remember. I have to spend the week at my aunt's, so I won't be around to remind you."

"I'll remember," I said.

"Okay," she said. "Well, I'd better go home now. Let me know if you need any help with Mrs. Townsend's gardens."

"I won't," I said for about the tenth time. "Need help, that is. But thanks anyway."

"See you," she said, and walked up her front walk. I kept walking until I reached my house and then went in. Mom was in the living room, rubbing her feet. She'd been rubbing her feet a lot ever since she started job hunting.

"Guess what?" I said. "I got another job. I'm going to take care of Mrs. Townsend's gardens while she's in the hospital."

"I didn't know she was sick," Mom said.

"Surgery," I said. "Isn't that great?"

"That she's in the hospital?" Mom asked. "Oh, you mean about your job. Yeah, I suppose so. But do you really know enough about gardening? Mrs. Townsend's gardens are beautiful."

"You're as bad as Lisa," I said. "I worked on our garden last summer, didn't I?"

"If I remember correctly, you were the one who refused to pull out any dandelions because they were so pretty," she said. "You said they couldn't possibly be weeds if they were so nice."

"Dandelions just have a bad reputation," I said. "How did the job-hunting go?"

"Nothing," she said, and rubbed her feet even harder. "They're not even polite anymore."

"What do you think you're going to do?" I asked and sat down on the arm of her chair. Mom looked awfully tired.

"Well, I'm going to quit this searching for a while," she said. "Before I'm completely crippled. Besides, I could use a bit of a vacation. Maybe I could convince your father that we should all go away for a while. We could see the Rockies or someplace like that."

"I can't leave Kid Power," I said. "And I don't think Carol'll want to give up her newspaper route. And you know how Dad feels about traveling."

"Fine," she said. "I'll go alone. Just as soon as the swelling goes down."

"You wouldn't really, would you?" I asked. Somehow I couldn't picture Mom enjoying herself looking at the

Rockies all by herself, but I'd never seen her unemployed before. Let alone unemployed with swollen feet.

Mom sighed. "I don't really feel like going anyplace right now except maybe the shower," she said. "I'm sorry to be so crotchety, but there's only so much rejection I can take in a single day."

"I understand," I said, and kissed her on the cheek. "Want me to make supper?"

"Would you, honey?" she asked. "I thought we might have tuna salad tonight."

"Sure," I said. Tuna salad was my specialty. "You go up and take a shower, and by the time you come down, supper'll be ready."

"That sounds wonderful," she said. "You are a magnificent daughter."

I smiled at her and got up. Just as I did, the phone rang.

"It couldn't possibly be for me," Mom said. "Answer it, hon."

So I did. "Hello?"

"Is this Kid Power?" a woman asked. She sounded kind of frenzied.

"Yes, it is," I said. "What can I do for you?"

"This might sound sort of strange," the woman said. "But your sign said 'No job too big or small.' "

"That's right," I said.

"My cat has to go to the veterinarian," the woman said. "And he's just terrified. I've been chasing him around the house all day, and right now he's hiding in the basement and I can't get him out, and even if I did, he wouldn't get into his carrying case and I don't know what to do. Could you help me?"

"I sure can," I said. "What's your address?"

"Fourteen Highland Avenue," the woman said. "Please hurry."

"I'll be there in a minute," I said. "In the meantime, stop chasing him around. You're just overexciting him."

"All right," the woman said. "Thank you."

I hung up. "Supper'll be a little late," I said to Mom. "I just got an emergency call. I have to get a cat into his carrier."

"Don't get scratched," she said, and flopped out in the chair. I kissed her good-bye, and ran down the block. Highland Avenue was a couple of blocks away, and I sprinted the distance. I would have preferred to walk to give me time to figure out a way of getting some dumb cat into his dumb carrier, but it was an emergency. I found number fourteen and rang the bell. A woman opened the door.

"Hi," I said. "I'm Janie Golden from Kid Power."

"I'm Mrs. Blake," the woman said. "My cat's still in the basement. I've tried calling to him, but he won't budge. I've already called the vet to say I'll be late, but I simply have to get him there before five."

I looked at my watch. "That gives us plenty of time," I said. "Where's the carrier?"

"On the kitchen table," she said. "I just had him in it when he realized what was happening, and he made a run for the basement. I'd forgotten the basement door was open. There are a thousand hiding places there. I couldn't possibly find him there unless he wants to be found."

"What's the cat's name?" I asked. Somehow that seemed a sensible question to ask.

"Peachy," the woman said. "I've had him for ten years now. He's always hated going to the vet's."

My father's allergic to cats and dogs, which is why we've never had any. But Grandma's had cats, so I know something about them. "What does your cat like to eat?" I asked.

"Cat's Cravings Cat Food," she said. "Peachy just loves their tuna flavor."

"Does Peachy like to eat?" I asked.

"He loves to," Mrs. Blake said. "Why?"

"Where's your can opener?" I asked.

"On the counter," she said.

I walked over to the counter. "Make sure the basement door is open," I instructed her. "And if Peachy comes out, make sure you close it fast." I pressed down on the can opener and listened while it made its whirring sound.

Sure enough, a fat orange cat bounded up the basement steps and into the kitchen. Mrs. Blake slammed the basement door behind him, but Peachy realized he'd been tricked, and ran away from both of us up the stairs.

"At least he's out of the basement," Mrs. Blake said, wiping the sweat from her forehead. "I should have thought about that can opener trick."

"My grandmother does it when she wants to get her cat in from outside," I said. "Where do you think Peachy's gone to now?"

"Probably under a bed someplace," Mrs. Blake said. "Should I take the carrier upstairs?"

I looked at it. Frankly, if I'd been Peachy I wouldn't have wanted to get into it either. It was a cardboard container with ugly cats sketched on it, and some holes for air. "I don't suppose you have anything else you could carry Peachy in?" I asked.

"What do you mean?" she asked and looked at the ceiling as though Peachy might fall through it and land in the carrier.

"A box or bag," I said. "Something he doesn't associate with going to the vet's."

"He does like playing in grocery bags," she said. "I never thought of taking him anyplace in one though."

"It's worth a try," I said. "The vet's isn't very far away, is it?"

"Just a few blocks," she said. "Peachy should be all right in a bag for that long."

"Good," I said. "Does Peachy like catnip?"

"Janie, I think you're a genius," Mrs. Blake said, and walked over to her kitchen cabinets. Out of one she took a grocery bag, out of another a box of catnip. We tip-toed upstairs, trying not to alarm Peachy, but it didn't work. He was waiting at the top of the stairs, and as soon as he saw us, he ran into one of the bedrooms. I ran after him, hoping I could catch up but I couldn't. It didn't seem fair somehow. My legs were longer than his.

I found him in the second bedroom I looked in. He was hiding under a double bed, right in the middle where it was too far to reach in and grab him. I couldn't be sure, but it looked like he was grinning at me.

"My poor kitten," Mrs. Blake said as she came into the bedroom. "The poor darling is so terrified."

Peachy didn't look the least bit terrified to me, but maybe he was the sort of cat who hid his feelings. "Let

me have the catnip," I said. "Do you mind if I spill some of it onto the floor?"

"Anything," she said, and handed me the box. "What should I do with the bag?"

"Put it down by the side of the bed," I said and got back on the floor. I stared in at Peachy. He winked at me.

I shook a little bit of the catnip between Peachy and me. If he fell for the can opener trick, I had the feeling he wasn't too bright and he'd probably fall for the old catnip ruse as well. He did.

He edged over to the catnip and ate it. I sprinkled a little more, again between him and me. He slid over to it, and ate it as well.

He was close enough to me so I could reach under the bed and grab him, but I decided to hedge my bet. First I sprinkled a lot of catnip into the shopping bag, and then I rested it on its side. Then I sprinkled some catnip right at the edge of the bed.

Peachy thought about it, and then greed overcame him. He poked his head out and sniffed around until he located the catnip. Just as he started to eat it, I started petting his back. I could hear him purr.

I grabbed him carefully under his belly, and before he knew what hit him, I put him in the bag and put the bag upright. Mrs. Blake rushed over and took the bag from me. She held it tightly on top, so that Peachy couldn't climb out, but loose enough so air could get in. I don't think he would have wanted to climb out anyway. He was purring pretty loud by then.

"I don't know how to thank you," Mrs. Blake said as

she carried Peachy downstairs. I could hear his purring turn into gentle snores.

"It's okay," I said. "That's what Kid Power is for."

We went back to her kitchen, and while she held Peachy in his bag, she fumbled with her pocketbook and took out her wallet. "Here," she said and handed me two dollars. "Thank you for a job well done."

"I only charge a dollar," I said, and tried to give her one of the bills back.

"Keep it," she said. "You deserve it, and besides I don't have time to argue. Thank you, Janie."

"Thank you," I said, and opened the kitchen door for her. She walked over to her car, and I started back for home. Two dollars for chasing a cat around for ten minutes. No wonder people become animal trainers.

Chapter Five

Mrs. Blake called me the next morning to thank me again and ask if I could come over every morning for a week to help her get five pills down Peachy's throat. That's what the vet had prescribed for him, and Mr. Blake wouldn't help at all. "He gets nervous around Peachy," Mrs. Blake said. I felt a little guilty charging a dollar a morning, but Mrs. Blake remembered that was my rate and offered to pay it, so I said sure. I made a point of stopping on my way to Mrs. Blake's to see if Mrs. Edwards needed anything. Mrs. Edwards usually didn't, but I could tell she was glad for the company, and I made a point of staying for a little bit and visiting. I'd always liked Mrs. Edwards, and I enjoyed talking to her. She told me she was glad to have somebody checking on her daily as well.

So I decided that when I stopped Kid Power, and I figured I probably would when school started, I'd make sure to check on Mrs. Edwards anyway. I didn't tell anybody about my resolution, but it made me feel better when she gave me my money at the end of each week.

With the $7.00 I'd earn from Mrs. Blake and the $2.50 from Mrs. Edwards, and $2.00 from Mrs. Marks for working on Harriet's wardrobe (my grandmother never made me clothes that nice) and $5.00 from Mr. Townsend, that was a practically guaranteed $17.50 in a single week. Of course some of the jobs I liked more than the others. Mrs. Edwards was always fun; she was my favorite. Getting Peachy to take his pills was kind of a drag. Mrs. Blake held him down, and I shoved the pills down his throat, then rubbed his neck to make sure he'd swallow, only sometimes he wouldn't, and I'd have to keep shoving and rubbing. It never took more than ten or fifteen minutes, but I earned my dollar. Peachy was even worse than I was about taking medicine, and I hate taking medicine.

I didn't much like working for Mrs. Marks. I resented all that modeling, and the more I heard about Harriet, the less I liked her. She got A's in everything, and was a Girl Scout, and won her school spelling bee three years in a row. I complained one night to Mom about Harriet, and Mom said she was sure that when Grandma talked about me, I was every bit as perfect-sounding, but that was no comfort. Harriet didn't have to put up with Grandma, after all.

But it wasn't even listening about Harriet that bothered me so much. It was a feeling of being used somehow. For fifty cents an hour, I stood around while Mrs. Marks pretended I was her granddaughter. I tried to explain how I felt at supper one night, but Dad decided I was being exploited and used it as an excuse to tell Carol and me again about the struggles of the working classes.

Saturday morning the phone rang, and I picked it up. "Hello?" I said. I'd been adding up my money for that week, my favorite Kid Power job.

"Is this Kid Power?" a woman asked.

"It is," I said and felt that little rush in my stomach I always got when someone new called.

"Do you do dog walking?" she asked.

"Sure," I said, still feeling good about Peachy. Sure, he was a cat, but an animal was an animal.

"Oh good," the woman said. "I need someone to walk my dog twice a day for the next week. Ten minutes a walk. Can you manage that?"

"Certainly," I said. "That'll be a dollar a day."

"Fine," the woman said. "My name is Mrs. Hodges, and I'm at 22 Lincoln Drive."

I wrote down the address.

"Why don't you come over at one?" she said.

"Fine," I said and hung up. I spent the rest of the morning doing nothing. It felt good after all my activity.

At 12:45 I left for Mrs. Hodges', and I arrived there right on time. With a ten-speed bike, I'd be able to get to my different jobs much faster. That certainly was an argument for using the money I'd be earning for a new bike.

Mrs. Hodges let me in. "Sugar is feeling a little chipper right now," she said. "A little frisky, but you should be able to control her. She just loves people."

I immediately got nervous. I don't know that much

about dogs. My father's allergic to everything except goldfish, and Gran only had cats. I'd thought Sugar was going to be one of those cute little dogs, a poodle maybe, but instead she turned out to be nearly as big as I was. She also bore a strong resemblance to a wolf.

"Nice sized dog you have there," I said, trying to sound unscared.

Mrs. Hodges put the leash on Sugar and handed her over to me. "She really is very fond of people," she said. "But she doesn't like other dogs very much. So if you can avoid any contact with them, do."

"Sure," I said, and took the leash. We went out the back door, and walked on the driveway to the sidewalk. I didn't much care which direction we went in, so I let Sugar pick. She chose right, so I went with her. Every few feet she paused and sniffed bushes, trees, or the ground. She went to the bathroom twice and sniffed some more after that. I had just about decided it was time to turn around and go back, and was trying to figure out the best way of convincing Sugar of that, when across the street, a little Scottish terrier spotted Sugar and me.

"It's okay," I said to Sugar and tried to turn her around.

But it was too late. The scottie crossed the street barking frantically and jumped on Sugar. The two dogs started screaming and fighting.

I pulled on Sugar's leash, but she broke away from me. I thought she'd kill the scottie, they were fighting so hard.

At first I just stood there not knowing what to do. I

was scared to jump in and pull the dogs apart. What if one of them bit me? Or both of them? I didn't know what dogs did when they got mad, but I was sure it wasn't pleasant.

So I shouted "Help!"

Sure enough, a man came charging out of the house the scottie had been in front of. "Ginger!" he cried and ran across the street. He jumped right in and pulled the dogs apart. He grabbed Ginger and held her, then untangled Sugar from her leash, which he gave me. "You stupid dog," he said to Ginger, while I tried to get Sugar under control.

"Ginger jumped right on her," I said. "Sugar was just minding her own business."

"I don't doubt it," he said. "Ginger gets very upset when she sees another dog. I shouldn't have let her out untied."

"It's okay," I said.

"They both seem to be all right," he said. "No harm done. I'm sorry if Ginger scared you."

"That's okay," I said, even though I was still trembling. I pulled on Sugar's leash and dragged her back to Mrs. Hodges. What if Ginger had been a big dog, as big as Sugar? She could have killed her, and I wouldn't have known what to do to stop them.

I got back to Mrs. Hodges as fast as I could, and handed Sugar back to her. I didn't even go in. "I can't handle this job," I said. "Sugar's just too big for me."

"Are you sure?" Mrs. Hodges asked.

"Positive," I said, even though it was the first job Kid Power had turned down, and I felt perfectly miserable about giving up seven dollars.

"Well, let me give you what I owe you," she said.

"No, that's okay," I said. I didn't feel I deserved it anyway, since I hadn't been able to keep Sugar out of a fight. Instead I ran home. Running made me feel better, and by the time I got home I felt almost okay. Just a little bit shaky.

"Lisa called about fifteen minutes ago," Mom told me when I got in. "She was very upset about something."

"Did she say what?" I asked.

"She didn't say," Mom said. "But I'd call her if I were you."

So I did. "Hi, Lisa," I said to her when she picked up the phone. "Did you have a good time at your aunt's?"

"Some friend you are," she said bitterly.

"What do you mean by that?" I asked nervously.

"We were supposed to go to the movies today, re-member?" she said.

"We were?" I asked, and thought about it. "Oh that's right, we were. I forgot all about it."

"I called you to remind you, but your mother said you were out."

"I was," I said. "I was walking a dog for Kid Power."

"I don't care about Kid Power. I don't care how much stupid money you make!" Lisa said. "Isn't it more im-portant we were supposed to go to the movies together? Isn't friendship more important than money?"

I knew she'd been waiting to shout that at me. I think of great things like that to say sometimes, but I usually don't have the chance or forget what I'm supposed to say when the chance comes. "Calm down Lisa," I said. "I forgot. I'm sorry. How was the movie?"

"I didn't go," she grumbled.

"No? Why not?"

"Because I would have had to take my brother," she said. "And he would have cried and made an idiot of himself, and I would have had to take him home right in the middle of the movie, and Mom would have blamed me for taking him to a scary movie in the first place. That's why."

"I'm really sorry I forgot," I said. "Can we go next week?"

"You'll probably be too busy next week," she said. "Making more precious money."

"Oh, cut it out," I said. "You're just jealous because I'm taking care of Mrs. Townsend's garden and you're not."

"I am not jealous," she said. "I thought you were my best friend."

"I am your best friend," I said.

"Then how come you forgot all about me?" she asked.

"You've forgotten about me too sometimes," I said.

"I never have," she said. "Name once when I forgot about you."

I thought about it for a moment. Lisa never forgot anything. When we were seven, I told her red was my favorite color, and when I was ten, she gave me a red pen for my birthday. Just because it was my favorite color. By then green was my favorite color, but I never had the heart to tell her. "So you have a better memory than I have," I said. "That doesn't mean I'm not your best friend."

"Face it, Janie," Lisa said. "All you care about is making money. That's all you ever talk about anymore. Money, money, money. You're a regular old Midas."

"I am not," I said.

"You are too," she said. "Go count your money and see how much fun that is."

"You're just jealous," I said again.

"I'll tell you one thing I'm not jealous of," she said. "There's something I think you should know."

"What?" I asked, more scared than mad.

"Remember those bugs you thought were so cute?" Lisa said. "They're Japanese beetles. They're going to eat Mrs. Townsend's garden until it's nothing but holes, and then you'll be sorry. Good-bye, Janie."

"Good-bye to you, too," I said angrily, and slammed down the phone. Mom, who'd been sitting in the kitchen pretending not to be listening, stopped pretending. "You two have a fight?" she asked.

"Shut up," I said, and stormed out of the kitchen. I went up to my room and looked at the envelope where I'd been keeping my money. I had wanted to count it, just to see how much I'd earned, but thanks to Lisa, I was no longer in the mood. So instead I stayed in my room until suppertime and read. I didn't enjoy it very much because every time the story got boring, I started thinking about Lisa. I almost called her again, but then I decided not to. Let her call. She was the one who insulted me. I hadn't said anything except to apologize. If she was any kind of friend, she'd just laugh and say it was okay. Let her be the one to call.

"You seem sulky tonight," Dad said at suppertime. We were having a barbecue, and he made the hamburgers. Dad always got upset when he did the cooking and we didn't eat enough.

"Lisa's mad at me," I said.

Dad looked at Mom. I recognized the old raised eye-brow look. "What about?" he asked.

I knew I didn't want to tell him, but I figured he'd worm it out of me. "She's just jealous because of Kid Power," I said.

"Lisa never seemed like the jealous type to me," Carol said.

"A lot you know," I said. "She's even jealous that I have an older sister."

"That's not jealousy, that's taste," Carol said.

"How did this fight happen?" Dad asked. "How do you know she's jealous?"

"We were supposed to go to the movies today and I forgot," I said. "I called her up when I got home, and I apologized for forgetting. I apologized a lot, but she didn't care. It's all because I got the job taking care of Mrs. Townsend's garden. She felt she should have gotten it because she knows more about gardening than I do."

"Then why don't you offer her the job?" Dad asked. "If she'd be good at it anyway . . ."

"Because it's my job!" I shouted. "I'm the one who made the posters."

"Well, actually I made the posters," Carol said.

Sometimes I really hate Carol. "It was my idea," I said. "I'm the one who's been working all summer to earn money for a bike, not Lisa. Why should I just give her a job?"

"Because she's your friend," Dad said. "And her friendship is worth more than a silly job. More than any money you might earn from it."

"You're just saying that because you don't like me working," I said. "You want me to give up all my jobs."

"I don't like you going around the whole neighborhood crying poverty, I admit that," he said.

"I did that once," I said. "Before I knew you didn't want me to do it. I wish you'd forget it. The people who call me now are perfect strangers."

"I'm not crazy about you working for perfect strangers either," he said. "There are a lot of strange people around. You might get into some kind of trouble."

"You don't like it when I work for people we know. You don't like it when I work for strangers," I said. "You just don't like it that I work."

"No I don't," he said. "I don't see the point to it. If you want the bike that much, we'll just buy you one. There's no reason for you to spend your childhood working all the time."

"It's not bad practice," Mom said. "After all, most women do have jobs nowadays."

"You don't seem to anymore," he said.

"Now what's that supposed to mean?" Mom asked.

"You haven't left the house in three days," he said. "You haven't even checked the want ads out. All you keep doing is muttering about your feet."

"They hurt!" Mom shouted. "You try getting a job this time of year and see how your feet feel about it."

"You haven't even made any phone calls," he said. "What's the matter, couldn't take the rejection?"

"No, I couldn't," Mom said. "Besides, why are you suddenly so desperate for me to get a job? It seems to me it took quite a while to convince you that I should even go back to school for my master's."

"That was different," Dad said. "The kids were little . . ."

"You don't have to use the same old excuses all over again," Mom said. "I remember each and every one of them."

"I suppose I'll get to listen to a whole new batch this summer," Dad said. " 'My feet hurt. It's hot outside. Nobody's hiring anyway.' " He mimicked Mom's voice.

"They're all true," Mom said. "My feet do hurt. It is hot outside. And nobody is hiring."

"If you wanted a job bad enough, you'd find one," Dad said.

"Don't be so simplistic!" Mom cried and left. We could hear her stomping her bad feet all the way upstairs.

Carol sat at the picnic table, carefully examining the sky. I tried to sit very still and disappear, but I accidentally moved my head and found Dad staring straight at me. He didn't have to say a word for me to know that somehow he blamed me for everything that was happening. And I almost couldn't blame him for blaming me.

Chapter Six

Mom spent Sunday making a point of reading every single want ad in the classified section. The really bad ones she read out loud to Dad, who grumbled until it was time for a baseball game. He turned one on as soon as he possibly could and refused to even pretend to listen to anybody after that.

Carol stayed in her room all day, after she'd delivered her papers. I went in to visit her at one point, and she told me flat out that the whole thing was all my fault, and if it wasn't for me, she'd have her new bike already and Mom and Dad wouldn't be quarreling and she wouldn't have to be hiding in her unairconditioned bedroom on a hot Sunday in July. She gave me the feeling she didn't really want to talk, so I left and went into Mom and Dad's bedroom. Mom was making a point of sitting in the living room with Dad, even if he wasn't talking to her, so there was plenty of privacy. I called every single one of my friends who was home for the summer except Lisa. There weren't that many of them. Most of my friends were in camp, which had just started, or else on trips with their parents or visiting their grandparents, but there were three left, and I called them all. Sheila said Kid Power sounded like a good idea; she'd like to earn some money, but her mother would never let her put her phone number anyplace public. Her mother had an unlisted phone number. Every time she had a crisis, she had the number changed. Sometimes it was impossible to reach Sheila for weeks. Ted said Kid Power sounded like a good idea, except he wouldn't want to do anything that would take too much time away from his baseball practice. Ted wants to be another Catfish Hunter when he grows up. And Margie said Kid Power sounded like a good idea except the only thing she could really do was babysit. That she's good at because she has three younger brothers and sisters so she's had lots of practice. None of them was the least bit interested in gross and net or how much money I had made or whether I should raise the rate for the oatmeal cookies at yard sales. It really made me appreciate Lisa. Besides, there was no one else I could turn to about those beetles. So I called her up, in spite of all my resolutions. She picked up the phone, and it took all my nerve to say, "Hi, Lisa," after I heard her say "Hello?"

"Oh it's you," Lisa said. "I'm still not talking to you." And she hung up.

I went downstairs after that and sat in silence with Dad watching the ballgame. Fortunately it was a doubleheader, so except for Mom occasionally calling out to us, "Wanted: Egg Processor. Good Hours. Call 264-9087,"

I was able to sit and look at the ballplayers and not think about anything at all.

The second game of the doubleheader went into extra innings. At some point during it Mom went into the kitchen and made herself a salad. Carol came downstairs and opened up a can of tuna fish. She didn't bother putting it on a plate, just ate it right out of the can. Nobody even told her to drain out the oil. Dad and I shared a big bag of potato chips.

"All natural," Dad muttered. "Lots of nutrition in potato chips."

It was the only thing he said all day.

I spent the next morning working hard. First I went over to Mrs. Blake's and helped her cure Peachy, who bit me. Then I went over to Mrs. Edwards' and visited for two hours. She didn't need anything, but she seemed glad to have my company, and I was glad not to be at home.

After I left Mrs. Edwards, I went to Mrs. Townsend's garden and checked out the Japanese beetles. Sure enough, they were eating all the leaves and flowers. The leaves looked like doilies. The roses just looked lousy.

Part of me just wanted to run as far away as I could from there and let the beetles do their worst, but I knew I couldn't give up without a fight. I owed that much to the Townsends. The problem was that even though I was considerably bigger than the beetles, they outnumbered me about a thousand to one. And I didn't know how to get rid of so many.

I picked one up and put it in the palm of my hand. I took my other hand and tried to squoosh the bug to

death, but even though I tried pretty hard, I didn't hurt the bug at all. I did feel sick to my stomach though. It was such a pretty bug. I'm good at killing mosquitoes, but this thing was harder and better-looking and had never stung me.

I threw the bug onto the ground and stomped on it. That worked, and I could see its mangled and bloody body right by my foot. I shuddered and moved away from it.

The only way I could see to get rid of the other 999 bugs would be to pick each one up and stomp it to death. I knew that was what I should do, but I couldn't. And I couldn't make myself do it. I followed my instincts and got out of there, leaving the beetles behind to eat away.

I didn't feel like going home for lunch, so I went to the bank to start a savings account. Everybody was very nice to me, but they said I had to have my parents' permission to save my own money. They didn't care that I'd earned the money all by myself, or that I'd read *A Child's First Book of Investments*. I was a minor, and that's all they cared about. So I took my money home with me and decided I'd ask Mom and Dad about a savings account when they were in better moods.

Mom wasn't in when I got home, which I took to be a good sign. At least it meant her feet hurt less. I drank some water and then I turned on the TV and watched a woman win ten thousand dollars in ten minutes on a game show. I thought about taking down the address of the show to see if I could be a contestant. Ten thousand dollars would sure solve a lot of problems. It would even pay for Mrs. Townsend's garden. I was pretty sure that I'd have to, once she got home and discovered how I'd wrecked it. It would probably take all the money I'd earned to pay for it. There went the bike. I wondered if Dad would give me matching funds to keep me from being sued.

I turned the TV off when I heard Mom come in. "Hi," I said, and tried to smile. "How was the job-hunting?"

"I wasn't job-hunting," she said. "I was at the movies."

I stopped smiling.

"Not you, too," she said. "Listen, you heard me read the want ads yesterday. There's nothing, nothing. Do you hear me? Absolutely nothing. So why should I kill myself trying to find a nonexistent job? I'm not even that sure I want to continue in social work."

"I thought you liked it," I said.

"Maybe I did," she said. "And maybe not. What does it matter?"

"It matters," I said, hoping Mom wouldn't expect me to say why it mattered. Fortunately, the phone rang. I looked at her to see if I should answer it.

"Your public awaits," she said. "Go, answer."

So I went to the phone and said, "Hello?"

"Hello, Janie? This is Mrs. Marks."

"Oh, hello Mrs. Marks," I said. Right then, even pretending to be Harriet sounded better than staying at home.

"I just heard the most wonderful news," she said. "My granddaughter Harriet is coming for a week's visit. Isn't that lovely?"

"It sure is," I said, trying to sound enthusiastic. A solid

week of perfection didn't sound so great to me, but then again I wasn't related to it.

"She's coming on Monday," Mrs. Marks said. "I do hope you can work me into your schedule this week. I'd love to have Harriet's new wardrobe ready for her when she arrives."

"I have lots of free time in the afternoons," I said.

"Marvelous," she said. "And do you think you could spend some time with Harriet when she's here next week? I thought she'd enjoy spending some time with girls her own age. Do you think you could show Harriet around, introduce her to your friends?"

"I guess so," I said. It was bound to be better than watching Mom and Dad fight.

"You're a sweetheart," Mrs. Marks said. "Could you come over right now, so we can get started on Harriet's clothes? I do want everything to be just perfect for her."

"I can come over," I said.

"Thank you, Janie," Mrs. Marks said. "And don't you worry, there'll be a special little bonus in it for you."

I had a feeling Harriet was going to be my special little bonus, but I didn't say anything. Instead I thanked her, and left for her house. Mom had turned the TV set on and was watching the same game show I'd had on before she came in. Somehow it didn't seem proper for her to be watching it, but I didn't say anything. Instead I went over to Mrs. Marks and stood still and didn't fidget while she put dresses on me, and pinned hems. I gave her a little bit of advice on trimmings, but mostly I listened while she told me some more about how wonderful Harriet was. By that point, I was almost curious about her. I'd never met a real angel before.

It was a long, bad week. There were no unexpected phone calls, no jobs from strangers, no yard sales, no surprises. Just Peachy and Mrs. Edwards and the Japanese beetles in the morning and Mrs. Marks in the afternoons. Even knowing I must be earning a lot of money with all that regular work didn't cheer me any. What was the point of the money, after all? I'd just be giving it to Mrs. Townsend, and then all that money I'd worked so hard for would be gone. And it seemed like all I was doing was working. Carol at least was swimming and seeing her friends and enjoying herself, but I was stuck at Mrs. Marks's every afternoon trying on clothes. I didn't like trying on clothes for myself, let alone for Harriet.

Evenings I spent at home. Mom and Dad were talking again, but they weren't saying very much, almost as though they were afraid if they started to talk they'd fight again. Everything on television was a rerun, which didn't help. I kept wanting to bring up the savings account, but the last thing I wanted was to start an argument. So all I could do was stuff my money in an envelope that was getting overloaded with quarters.

And Lisa didn't call. I certainly wasn't going to call her again, not after the way she hung up on me, but it really hurt that she hadn't called back to apologize. How long could she stay mad just because I forgot about that stupid movie? And I couldn't call anybody else because they all wanted to do things, and I didn't have any time for them. I knew things would be better after Harriet came, and I wouldn't have to work for Mrs. Marks anymore, but it was still a pain that week.

Everything was a pain that week. I decided making money was overrated. When I grew up, I'd stay at home and be a housewife. Let my husband support me. And if he didn't like it, I'd just divorce him and find another man who did. Not working ever again sounded like a wonderful way to live. I hardly blamed Mom anymore for having feet that hurt all the time.

Chapter Seven

Mrs. Marks invited me over to meet Harriet on Wednesday. I reminded her of my daily morning jobs, and she said that was fine, I should come over after lunch and take Harriet to my house. "The poor dear is getting tired of being with adults all the time," she said. "She could use the companionship of a girl her own age, especially such a nice girl like you."

I kept hoping for a last minute reprieve, an unexpected yard sale or an earthquake, but nothing happened, and I was just curious enough to be willing to meet Harriet. I told Carol the night before though that I was dreading spending the afternoon with her.

"Don't go then," she said.

I knew that was perfectly sensible advice, but I felt obliged somehow to go, mostly because I never told Mrs. Marks that I wouldn't. It seemed like those dinners Dad sometimes had with people he worked with. He didn't always like the people, but he said he had to socialize with them as part of the job. So on Wednesday afternoon I dressed up in a fresh pair of shorts and a T-shirt and went over to Mrs. Marks's.

She was delighted to see me. "Janie's here!" she called to Harriet. "Come in, dear," she said. "Harriet's just dying to meet you."

I doubted that, but I came in anyway. As I walked into the living room, Harriet came down the stairs. She was wearing a yellow pants suit that I had helped her grandmother to make. It seemed funny to see her wearing an outfit I'd worn so many times before. I grinned, half out of nervousness.

"Hi, Harriet," I said, trying to sound enthusiastic. "It's nice meeting you."

"Nice meeting you, too," Harriet said. She didn't look anything like me, but we were sort of built the same. The same height, and I guess the same weight. She had dark brown hair though, which she wore in two long pigtails on the sides of her head.

"Janie, would you like something to eat?" Mrs. Marks asked. She was always offering me stuff to eat when I was over helping her. She made a really good angel food cake.

"No thanks," I said. "I just had lunch." I kept staring at Harriet, wearing that pants suit. I wished I'd worn something better than shorts and a T-shirt.

"Why don't you take Harriet around and introduce her to your friends?" Mrs. Marks said, and gave Harriet a little push in my direction. "Harriet would enjoy that, wouldn't you dear?"

"Yes, Gran," Harriet said. "Come on, Janie."

"Okay," I said. "Good-bye, Mrs. Marks."

"Good-bye, dear," she said. "Have a nice afternoon."

"We will," Harriet said grimly, and we left the house.

I wished more than ever that Lisa and I were still speaking. Lisa was really good with new kids. I just got shy with them.

"So you're Janie," Harriet said, as we started walking toward my house.

"I am," I said, but that sounded really dumb. "So you're Harriet," I added. That sounded even dumber.

"Gran talks about you all the time," Harriet said. "She says you're hard-working and a credit to your parents and very sweet."

"She told me all about you, too," I said, only I didn't like the way that sounded either. I didn't want Harriet to think I agreed with Mrs. Marks about my being a credit to my parents and all that. "I'm really not a credit to my parents."

"I didn't think you were," she said. "What does Gran say about me?"

"How smart you are and all that," I said. "And how you're a Girl Scout."

Harriet snorted. "I haven't been a Girl Scout in years," she said. "Gran just doesn't remember I quit."

"I was a Brownie once but I didn't like it," I said. Lisa and I had joined together, but she stuck with it and I didn't. Oh, where was Lisa when I really needed her!

"You helped Gran with this outfit, didn't you?" Harriet asked. We were practically in front of my house and I didn't know what to do. Mom had been very unpredictable lately.

"Yeah," I said. "It looks good on you."

"Mom hates it when Gran makes clothes for me," Harriet said. "She's going to be really upset when I come home with a whole new wardrobe."

"Why doesn't your mother like it?" I asked.

"She thinks Gran thinks we don't have enough money to buy my own clothes," Harriet said. "She and Gran don't get along too great anyway. That's why I came out here alone."

"When you get home, will you wear the clothes Mrs. Marks made for you?" I asked.

"Probably not," Harriet said and shrugged. "Usually whenever I get stuff from Gran, Mom takes me on a shopping spree and buys me all new stuff. She says store-bought is better. And then I'll hang Gran's stuff in the closet and just forget to wear it until it's too small for me."

I thought about all the hours I'd put in trying on all of Harriet's dresses, and all the time Mrs. Marks had put in making them, and I really wanted to say something. But I knew it would be better if I didn't. "This is my house," I said instead. "Want to come in?"

"I guess so," Harriet said. "We have to spend at least a little time together or else Gran'll get upset."

I felt the same way as she did, but I at least was trying to act like I wanted to be with her. I resented the fact that Harriet wasn't willing to pretend, too.

We walked up the front steps and I opened the door. "Mom, are you home?" I called, but there was no answer. "Come on in," I said to Harriet. "My mother seems to be out right now."

"Okay," Harriet said and came in. "You have a nice house," she said, checking the living room out. "Who reads all those books?"

"We all do," I said. Our whole house is loaded with books, but I tend to forget they're there unless somebody points them out to me.

"You like to read?" she asked, picking one of the books up and looking at it.

"Yeah," I said. "I haven't had much chance to this summer though because of Kid Power."

"What's that?" she asked, still looking at the book.

"It's this organization I formed," I said. "I do it to earn money."

"Oh yeah, Gran mentioned it," Harriet said. "How come you have to earn money? Don't your folks have money for anything but books?"

"We have enough money," I said. "But Mom got laid off her job, so I thought I'd help out."

"Oh, that's right," she said. "A credit to your parents and all that."

"All that," I echoed. "Would you like to see my room?"

"Sure," she said, and put the book down. "Do you have any brothers or sisters?"

"An older sister," I said. "She's out now too, swimming. Carol swims a lot."

"I'm an only child," Harriet said. "Thank goodness."

"Having a sister isn't too bad," I said. If Harriet had criticized torture, I probably would have defended it at that point. We walked up the stairs and I showed her my room.

"Do you share it with your sister?" she asked as we walked in. I have a double bed, so there would be room for the two of us.

"Carol's room is across the hall," I said.

"You do have a lot of books," Harriet said, looking at my bookshelves. "You like mysteries?"

"They're my favorite," I said.

"Mine, too," she said, making me sorry I'd said I liked them. "What did you say about your sister's room?"

"It's right across the hall," I said.

"So if I stayed here nobody would bother me?" she asked.

"Nobody would bother you," I said.

"Okay then, that's what I'll do," Harriet said and took one of my books off the shelf. She sat down in my rocking chair. "I'll stay here and read for a while. I've always wanted to read this book."

"What do you want me to do?" I asked helplessly.

"I don't care," Harriet said. "Go out and earn some more money if you want. I just want to be alone and read for a while."

"For how long?" I asked.

"Until four," she said looking at my clock. "Then we can go back to Gran's."

"But don't you want to go out and do something?" I asked.

"Not particularly," she said. "I've been doing stuff all week. I'd rather read."

I didn't know what to say. Part of me was screaming that Harriet was invading my bedroom without even asking my permission, but another part of me thought it was a lot better than having to keep her company for two hours with nothing to say to her and not liking her one bit. This way everybody would be happy, me, Harriet, and especially Mrs. Marks. There were worse arrangements.

I guess Harriet could see I was hesitating. "Don't worry," she said. "I won't look at any of your precious stuff."

"I didn't think you would," I said coldly. "Okay, I'll knock on the door at four."

"Fine," Harriet said, and opened the book up. I left my room and closed my door behind me. I went downstairs and found a book to read. I wanted to sit on the back porch, but I was afraid somebody would see me alone and somehow Mrs. Marks would hear about it, so I stayed in the living room and started to read.

Mom came in a half an hour later. "Hi honey," she said. "Help me with these groceries, would you?"

"Sure," I said, and took the bags from her. We walked into the kitchen together, each carrying a bag.

"I thought you were going to be spending the afternoon with Harriet," Mom said as we put the bags down on the counter.

"I am," I said. "She's up in my room reading."

"She is?" Mom said. "Did you two have a fight?"

"I don't think so," I said. "She just wanted to be alone and read."

"Oh, all right," Mom said, and started putting stuff in the refrigerator. "Would she like to stay and have supper with us?"

"No, she wants to go back to her grandmother's at

four," I said. "Mom, she never wears the clothes Mrs. Marks makes for her."

"She doesn't?" Mom said. I had a strong feeling she wasn't listening to me.

"None of them," I said. "With all the work Mrs. Marks does, she doesn't even wear them. Her mother doesn't like her to."

"Grandmothers and mothers don't always get along," Mom said. "I thought I'd make tuna noodle casserole for supper tonight. What do you think?"

"Tuna noodle casserole sounds fine," I said with a sigh. Mom hadn't listened well when she was studying for final exams or writing papers for college either. She was always too "distracted." Now she was distracted because there was nothing distracting her except tuna noodle casserole.

"I'm going into the living room," I said.

"Why not sit on the back porch?" she asked. "I'm going to just as soon as I put all the groceries away."

"I don't think so," I said. "I'll see you later."

"Sure, hon," she said.

I read until ten of four, then spent five minutes working my nerve up to go to my own room and knock on my own door. I finally got indignant enough not to be scared and went upstairs.

"Come in," Harriet said after I knocked, so I did.

"It's time," I said.

"Okay," she said, getting up. "I didn't have a chance to finish the book," she said. "I'll take it with me and give it to Gran to give back to you when I've finished."

"Okay," I said. I guessed it was okay, too. What harm would it do to loan her a book? "We'd better get going."

"All right," she said.

"My mom wanted to know if you'd like to have supper here," I said.

"It would break Gran's heart if I did," she said, and started downstairs. "Thank your mother for the invitation though."

"I will," I said, following her down. We left the house and walked to Mrs. Marks's in silence. Harriet held on tightly to my book.

"We're almost there," she said to me when we reached Mrs. Marks's block. "Come on, start talking."

"About what?" I asked.

"Anything," Harriet said. "Just so Gran thinks we spent all our time talking."

"Oh," I said. "So what are your favorite subjects, Harriet?" Adults always ask me that when they can't think of anything else to say.

"English," she said. "And social studies."

English and social studies were my favorite subjects, too. It was amazing how much Harriet and I had in common and how horrible she was. "I like them, too," I said, and couldn't think of another polite thing to say.

"Are you excited about starting junior high?" she asked.

"I guess so," I said, relieved to reach the front door. "Carol seems to enjoy it."

"I wish I had a sister," Harriet said loudly and rang the bell. I just stared at her. "Hi Gran," she said, as Mrs. Marks opened the door for us. "Did you have a nice afternoon?"

"Very nice," Mrs. Marks said, and kissed Harriet on the cheek. "Did you girls enjoy yourselves?"

"We had a great time," Harriet said. "Too bad we don't have any more time to spend together."

"It is a shame," Mrs. Marks said. "Well Janie, would you like to come in and tell me what you girls did?"

I swallowed hard. "I'd love to," I said. "But my mom's expecting me home to help her with supper."

"Janie's mom invited me to stay for supper," Harriet said. "But I said I wanted to eat with you more."

"You should have had dinner with your new friend," Mrs. Marks protested, but she was beaming. I had to hand it to Harriet. She was the single best liar I'd ever met.

"Well, I've got to be going," I said, eager to get home.

"Harriet, would you be a darling and get my glasses for me?" Mrs. Marks said. "I think I left them on the kitchen table."

"Sure, Gran," Harriet said. "Bye, Janie."

"Good-bye," I said and watched her leave.

Mrs. Marks took an envelope out of her skirt pocket. "Here, Janie," she said. "That little bonus I promised you."

"Thank you," I said and took the envelope from her. I didn't even think about what might be in it, I was so eager to escape.

"You've been an angel," Mrs. Marks said. "Harriet and I both appreciate it."

"Okay," I said. "Well, good-bye Mrs. Marks."

"Good-bye, dear," she said, and closed the door. I walked down her front steps and all the way to the end of the block before I thought about opening the en-

velope and seeing what was in it. I stood at the inter-
section and ripped the envelope open. In it was a five
dollar bill. No note or anything. Just money for spending the afternoon with Harriet and pretending to like
her.

I understood then what people meant when they
called it dirty money.

Chapter Eight

Whether I wanted to or not, I was committed to keeping Kid Power going, at least until Mrs. Townsend came back from the hospital and sued me. So I gritted my teeth and kept earning money. By that point I couldn't have cared less about getting a new bike. I'd never been all that crazy for one anyway; it was always more Carol's idea than mine. There was nothing I really wanted at that point except my freedom and a job for Mom. And Kid Power could supply me with neither.

At least my work with Mrs. Marks was over with. A couple of weeks earlier I would have been upset to lose all that money coming in regularly, but a couple of weeks ago I hadn't lost my best friend or my self-respect. I wished a lot that it was a couple of weeks ago.

The only thing I really felt good about was visiting Mrs. Edwards. She was so nice to me. When I was in a hurry, she never made me stay and talk, the way Mrs. Marks did. And when I told her I was in no rush, she'd invite me to stay a while and talk to her about things. I wished I could tell her about Harriet, but it was a secret somehow, so I kept my mouth shut. I didn't tell her about how everybody in my family was constantly getting ready to shout at everybody else in my family either. And the Japanese beetles were something I preferred to keep to myself. But even with all those things I couldn't discuss, there was plenty for Mrs. Edwards and me to talk about. We talked about television a lot; we liked some of the same shows. We talked about school, since Mrs. Edwards used to be a schoolteacher. She liked hearing what things had changed and what was still the same. And I told her about getting Peachy to take his pills and who bought what at garage sales.

Another thing I liked about Mrs. Edwards was that she never gave me any extra money because I stayed and visited with her. Sometimes my visits lasted two hours, and even with her special senior citizen discount rate, that should have cost her a dollar. But I didn't want the extra money. I figured I was being paid fifty cents a day to see if she needed anything; the visits were all because I wanted to. Mrs. Edwards understood that without my saying anything. At the end of each week she gave me $2.50 and never a penny more. I liked that.

I used to go over first thing every morning, since Mrs. Edwards was an early riser, and if she wanted something, I figured she might as well get it as soon as possible. So Monday morning, a few days after Harriet's visit, I went over to check on Mrs. Edwards and see if I could pick up something for her. I had a feeling I probably could run an errand for her, because I knew she had library books due.

I walked over there and rang the doorbell, but there

was no answer, so I rang it again. There was still no answer. I decided I'd better knock on the door, since maybe the doorbell was broken. Our doorbell breaks all the time. Mom always calls it shoddy workmanship, but Dad refuses to, because of his respect for workmen. Dad's respect can drive you crazy.

There was still no answer, so I waited a couple of minutes, and then I rang the bell again. Nothing. I knocked on the door. Nothing. That meant that Mrs. Edwards wasn't in. If she'd been home, she might have been upstairs or in the bathroom or even in the cellar putting up preserves, but after all that time she would have heard the front door and had time to answer it. Which meant she was out.

So I went over to Mrs. Townsend's poor garden. Mr. Townsend had left me a new sheet of instructions on his back porch. There was mostly stuff about pruning this time. Pruning sounded good, since it meant I could cut away at least some of the branches the Japanese beetles had destroyed. I picked up the pruning shears, and started on the hedges.

Chopping the hedges down to size was actually kind of fun. Besides it felt good to know I was supposed to destroy things. And even if I cut the hedges too short, they'd grow back, and probably by the time Mrs. Townsend got back from the hospital. So I felt pretty good about what I was doing for a change.

I was hard at work when I heard someone say "hello" very softly. I looked up and saw Lisa.

"Hi," I said, cool and scared.

"I see you're trimming the hedges," she said.

"Yeah," I said. I thought about saying something nasty, but I didn't want to. "Do you think I'm doing it okay?"

"Just fine," Lisa said quickly. "You're a very good hedge trimmer."

"Thanks," I said.

"I was just walking by," she said. "And I saw you working and I thought I might as well come over and say hello."

"You might as well," I said. "I mean I'm glad you did."

"I'm glad I did, too," Lisa said and smiled. "Actually, I've been walking past Mrs. Townsend's garden practically every day for weeks now so I could come over and say hello."

"You didn't see me before this?" I asked. It seemed impossible. It felt like I'd been doing nothing but working on that garden since the end of school.

"I did," Lisa said. "At least three times. But I never had the nerve to come over. You must be pretty mad at me."

"No," I said truthfully. "I never should have forgotten about that movie. It was important to you."

"Kid Power's important to you," Lisa said. "Besides, I had no business hanging up on you."

"Well, that did bother me," I admitted. "But it doesn't matter. I missed you so much."

"I missed you even more," Lisa said. "It's been just horrible."

"I know," I said.

"So," Lisa said. "Have you been keeping busy?"

"I've been doing okay," I said. It felt strange talking to Lisa, and I could see she wasn't comfortable doing it either. I had a feeling the more we talked the better it would get. "Kid Power's been keeping me pretty busy, but lately things have slowed down."

"Have you made much money?"

"I guess so," I said. "I haven't added it up in a while."

"Did you start a savings account?" she asked.

"Not yet," I said. "The money's all stuffed in an envelope in my room."

"That's pretty stupid," Lisa said. "If it was in a bank, you'd be getting interest."

She said that very strictly, the way she always corrected me. I laughed. I never thought it would feel good to have Lisa correcting me, but it did.

Lisa looked puzzled for a little bit, and then she laughed, too. "I'm sorry," she said. "I'm always scolding you."

"I always deserve it," I said. "Well, not always. But often enough. I've been meaning to start a savings account, but I need one of my parents to come with me and sign the forms, and they've been so funny lately, I haven't wanted to ask."

"Your mom still doesn't have a job?" Lisa asked. I started clipping the hedges again.

"Not yet," I said. "And I don't think she ever will. She just sits around all day and reads. She buys every magazine she can find, and she reads them over and over again. Sometimes she even copies down recipes."

"That's terrible," Lisa said, shaking her head. "Does she at least cook what she copies?"

"Not yet," I said. "We've had tuna noodle casserole three times this week."

Lisa made a face. She hates tuna noodle casserole. I used to like it, but after three times in one week, I'd lost my appetite for it as well. The last time she served it, Dad looked like he wanted to throw it at someone, but instead he just had a couple of bitefuls and left the table. I used to like suppertime, but not anymore.

"What have you been up to?" I asked.

"Nothing much," Lisa said. "I've been helping my folks with our garden." She looked wistfully at Mrs. Townsend's.

"Lisa, I've just got to ask you," I said. "Have I wrecked everything here?"

"Wrecked it?" she asked. "What do you mean?"

"I've been so scared I've been weeding the flowers and fertilizing the weeds," I said. "And I know those stupid Japanese beetles have been eating everything. I even dream about them at night." I did too. I dreamt they ate my money just like they ate the roses, but I didn't want to tell Lisa that. "Is anything okay?"

Lisa walked around the garden slowly. I could see her inspecting each plant. My stomach turned over three times while she did.

"Well," she said, when she came back from her tour of inspection. "You do have a nice crop of ragweed growing."

"Oh, no," I said.

Lisa smiled. "Except for that, and the Japanese beetles, everything's fine," she said. "And it won't take more than a minute to pull out the ragweed." She pointed to where it was growing.

"I thought they were marigolds," I said faintly.

"They look alike," she said. "But they're not the same."

"Lisa, I hate this job," I said. "I never know what I'm doing, and it's a miracle I haven't destroyed everything."

"You're doing fine," Lisa said. "Much better than I thought you would."

"Would you please take it over for me?" I asked. "You know the difference between ragweed and marigolds. You'd be just perfect for it."

"But the Townsends hired you," Lisa said.

"They won't care," I said. "The important thing is that the garden be taken care of, not who does it."

"You sure you don't mind?" Lisa said. "I've really wanted to work on it. I just read about this wonderful way of killing Japanese beetles, and I've been dying to try it out."

"Oh, please try, Lisa," I said. "I'd be so grateful."

"Give me those pruning shears," she said. "You've been much too shy about cutting."

I handed them over to her and watched while she started chopping the branches off.

"My mother says never be bashful about pruning," Lisa said. "What're you doing this afternoon?"

"Nothing," I said, feeling shocked at how fast those hedges were losing their branches.

"Come on over to my place?" she asked. "We could talk."

"I'd love to," I said. "Lookit, I'd better go over

to Mrs. Edwards now and check on her. Do you mind if I leave you here?"

"Of course not," Lisa said. "I'll see you later."

"Okay," I said, feeling better than I had in ages. Lisa was my friend again, and I never had to worry about Mrs. Townsend's flowers. She was even going to kill the Japanese beetles. I decided that that night I'd ask my parents about a savings account. If I was in a good mood, it would help.

Mrs. Edwards still wasn't home. I wondered where she might have gone, but decided it was nothing to worry about. I went home and made myself a peanut butter and jelly sandwich for lunch. Mom was in the living room copying recipes.

"What're you doing?" I asked her, taking my sandwich into the living room.

"What does it look like?" she asked. "I'm copying recipes."

"Why?" I asked.

"So we can eat better balanced diets," she said. "And have more variety in our meals. That's why."

I thought about mentioning the tuna noodle casseroles, but decided against it.

"What're we having for supper?" I asked instead.

"I don't know," Mom said, busy copying the ingredients down. "Tuna noodle casserole maybe. We all like it."

"Oh," I said, and finished my sandwich fast. I went into the kitchen and made myself another one. I knew I wouldn't be eating much supper that night.

I ate my second sandwich and then washed the dishes.

I decided to go to Lisa's by way of Mrs. Edwards. I didn't want her to have any overdue library books.

I walked over there and rang the bell again. There was still no answer. I thought about leaving and trying again on my way back from Lisa's, but I decided to check things out first. So I went around back to see if maybe she was in her back yard. She wasn't. I didn't think she would be but it seemed worth checking.

I was sure Mrs. Edwards was just out someplace, but it seemed unlike her not to leave me a note or call me in the morning to say she wouldn't be home. I decided I'd better check a little more thoroughly.

Mrs. Edwards had those old-fashioned cellar doors, the kind that are outside the house, like Dorothy tries to open in *The Wizard of Oz* during the cyclone. I was pretty sure they wouldn't be locked, and they weren't. There was a regular door at the end of the stairs, and I opened that, too. Lots of people keep their cellar doors unlocked where I live.

I ran through the cellar, half-afraid I'd be arrested for breaking and entering, and climbed up the stairs to the kitchen. Once I got upstairs, I called Mrs. Edwards' name, but she didn't answer. I checked the kitchen, the dining room, and the living room, and still didn't see her. So I walked to the staircase, meaning to go upstairs and see if she was there. Except when I got to the hallway, I found her lying at the foot of the steps, her body sort of twisted.

At first I thought she was dead and I wanted to scream. But I made myself look carefully, and I could see she was still breathing. She was definitely unconscious. I wanted to move her, make her more comfortable, but I remembered you weren't supposed to move someone who'd been in an accident. Mrs. Edwards had probably fallen down the stairs first thing that morning. She was fully dressed.

I ran to the living room and took the afghan off the sofa and wrapped it around Mrs. Edwards as best I could without moving her. Then I went to the kitchen and found the phone book. I found the number for Hathaway Hospital, and I dialed it. While the phone was ringing, I took a deep breath.

"Hathaway Hospital," a woman's voice said.

"My name is Jane Golden," I said in my most adult voice. I was really scared they'd think I was a kid playing a practical joke. "I'm at 1082 North Thomas Street. There's been an accident here and I need an ambulance."

"What kind of accident?" the woman asked.

"The woman who lives here fell down the stairs. She's unconscious," I said.

"Don't move her," the woman said. "We'll send an ambulance right over."

I hung up the phone and called my mother. I knew I'd want to go to the hospital, and I doubted they'd let me go in the ambulance. Besides, I needed her. As soon as I told her what happened, she came right over.

The ambulance came right after her. Two men lifted Mrs. Edwards up very gently, and put her on a stretcher. They took her to the ambulance. The doctor asked me a couple of questions and I told him what I knew and what I'd guessed.

"You're a smart girl," he said when I told him what I'd done. "This woman may very well owe her life to you." He got into the ambulance and it drove off.

Mom and I followed it to the hospital. We waited in the emergency room for what seemed like hours. We talked about little things while we waited, and we watched other people coming in and leaving. We talked about everything except Mrs. Edwards.

After a while, another doctor came out. "Janie Golden?" she asked.

I stood up. "Yeah?" I said.

The doctor smiled. "Mrs. Edwards has a broken hip," she said. "She's in pain, but no danger, and she's regained consciousness. She said for me to come out and thank you."

"Can I see her?" I asked.

"Not now," the doctor said. "We have to get her to a room and start taking care of her. But she wants you to know how very grateful she is for your rescuing her."

"Thank you," I said, and watched as the doctor went back into Mrs. Edwards' cubicle.

"You can be proud," Mom said, getting up. "Well honey, I think we should go back now. There's nothing more we can do here."

"Okay," I said. "Oh my gosh."

"What is it?" Mom asked.

"I was supposed to see Lisa this afternoon," I said. "You don't think she'll get mad at me again for forgetting about her, do you?"

"I don't think so," Mom said and smiled. "I'm sure she'll understand when you explain you had something more important to do today."

Chapter Nine

I biked over to the hospital the next day to visit with Mrs. Edwards, but they wouldn't let me see her.

"What do you mean I can't see her?" I asked the nurse. "I rescued her."

"I understand that," the nurse said. "But rules are rules. No visitors allowed under the age of fifteen."

I might pass for fifteen on the telephone in an emergency, but there was no way I could claim to be that old in person. I started walking away dejectedly when a woman stopped me. She'd been in the corridor when the nurse and I were having our discussion.

"What do you mean you rescued her?" the woman asked. "What woman did you rescue?"

"Mrs. Edwards," I said. "And I didn't rescue her really. But I helped and it's not fair I can't see her. I'm sure she'd want to see me."

"My name is Liz Davis and I work for the *Hathaway Gazette*," she said, taking out her press card to show me. "I'd like to hear your story."

"Okay," I said, and soon we were sitting in the hospital lobby, while I explained to her about checking on Mrs. Edwards and finding her and calling the hospital. And that led to an explanation of why I was checking on Mrs. Edwards, and that led to my telling Ms. Davis all about Kid Power. She seemed very interested and took a lot of notes. I'd never been interviewed before for a real newspaper and hoped I was doing it right.

"That's a very interesting story," she said, once I'd finished. "Would you mind if I took a couple of pictures of you?"

"For the paper?" I asked.

"Absolutely," she said. "You're a heroine. People in this town would be interested in reading about you."

So we went to the parking lot and Ms. Davis took her camera out of her car, and I posed in front of the hospital for a few minutes. The sun was shining in my eyes and I tried not to squint.

"Well," Ms. Davis said when she finished taking pictures. "Don't be surprised if you see a story about yourself in the *Gazette* tomorrow."

"Tomorrow?" I said, surprised.

"Maybe the day after," Ms. Davis said. "But be on the lookout. You're going to be a celebrity pretty soon."

I thanked her and biked home. I was pretty excited about being a celebrity, but I decided not to tell my family until the story actually appeared. We got the *Gazette* because that was the paper Carol delivered. She made us get a subscription.

I was in everybody's good graces anyway because of how I found Mrs. Edwards. Dad and Mom were both proud of me, and Carol admitted I'd done well. I'd even brought up the subject of a savings account, and I was surprised at how agreeable Mom and Dad were about it.

"Of course you should have a savings account," Dad had said after supper. "I'm surprised you didn't ask for one earlier."

I didn't mention how risky it had been for weeks to bring up anything in that household, and as a result, I remained in everyone's good graces. Mom agreed to go with me to the bank just as soon as I wanted. I'd decided to go on Thursday because I wanted to have my books up to date before I went, and I hadn't been writing anything down in ages. I had a lot of catching up to do. Besides, I'd thought I'd have a chance to visit with Mrs. Edwards. Instead, I biked over to the five-and-ten and bought her a get-well card. I biked home by way of the Townsends' garden and found Lisa hard at work weeding.

"You missed some," she told me as I stopped to visit. "I'm making sure everything's perfect."

"I appreciate it," I said. "You know the garden doesn't look half-bad."

"You did a very good job except for the beetles," she said, shielding her eyes from the sun while she looked up at me. "Oh, speaking of jobs . . ."

"Yeah?" I said.

"I was telling my mother about how I was taking care of the garden . . ."

"She didn't mind, did she?" I asked nervously. There was no reason why Lisa's mother should mind, but my parents had been so crazy all summer, I was afraid it might be contagious with parents that year.

"No, of course not," Lisa said. "But she said I should ask you about money."

"Oh," I said. That sounded right. Lisa wouldn't ask me on her own and her mother would insist on it. "Gee, I don't know. I've been getting a dollar an hour."

"That's what I thought," Lisa said. "But I wouldn't expect all that."

"Why not?" I asked.

"I don't deserve it all," she said. "You found me this job, after all. It's like you're an agent."

Lisa's mother is an agent, so she knows about things like that. "How much does your mother get for finding people jobs?" I asked.

"Ten percent," Lisa answered.

I giggled. "Ten percent of a dollar is ten cents," I said. "I hope your mother's clients get more than a dollar an hour."

"They do," Lisa said. "Do you want more? Maybe a quarter an hour?"

"No, ten percent sounds okay," I said. "After all, I'm not doing any of the work. And besides, I think I'm going to quit Kid Power."

"Really?" she asked. "Why?"

"I've run out of jobs," I said. "Peachy is cured now, and you're taking care of Mrs. Townsend's garden. I was thinking about taking my sign down and just spending the rest of the summer loafing. And collecting my ten percent."

"But what about your bike?" she asked.

"I have my old one," I said. "Maybe I'll get a new one for my birthday."

"Ten percent then," Lisa said and wiped her hand off on her shorts so we could shake on the deal. We shook hands to make it official, and then we giggled again.

"Is this how your mother got started?" I asked.

"Not at ten cents an hour," she said.

I would have gone over to the supermarket then to get my sign except that it felt good to know I could go home and not worry too much, so I left Lisa and biked down to my place. I got a postage stamp, and wrote a note to Mrs. Edwards on the card, and mailed it. Then I brought my books up to date. I'd miss all those gross and nets once Kid Power was finished.

The next morning, I ran downstairs to get the paper first. Sure enough, there was an article about me on page five. I was squinting a little bit in the picture, but it didn't matter. The article told all about Kid Power and Mrs. Edwards, and it made me sound like a saint almost. If I hadn't known it was just me, I would have been very impressed.

I showed my parents the article (Carol was delivering the paper to other people), and they oohed and aahed, and Dad said he was going to pick up a half-dozen copies to send to my grandparents and for my scrapbook and for him to show off at his office. And then Grandma called, because she'd seen the article and she wanted to congratulate me, so I talked with her for a while. I tried to explain I wasn't nearly as wonderful as I sounded in the article, but she kept telling me not to be so modest, I was a wonderful girl, so bright not to have lost my head in an emergency, and very enterprising to boot. She sounded like Mrs. Marks talking about Harriet.

I no sooner hung up from Grandma when the phone started ringing again. My friends called to congratulate me, and Mrs. Marks called to say what a darling girl I was. Mrs. Blake called to say she was very proud of me and Peachy missed me all the time, which I doubted. Even the first lady I yard saled for called to say she'd read the article and was impressed that I'd kept Kid Power going. I didn't get off the telephone until lunchtime, when I made myself a tuna fish sandwich. As long as it didn't have noodles in it, I didn't mind.

That afternoon I got three more phone calls. Two were from ladies who wanted me to help them with their yard sales (the article said that was my specialty), and one woman wanted me to babysit. I told the yard sale ladies that I'd be delighted to and wrote the dates on the calendar. The babysitting lady I said I'd get back to. I would have liked to accept, but there was that family rule about my babysitting. So I brought it up at supper. I figured it would be safe, since everybody still liked me.

"I don't see why you can't sit," Mom said. "I think you're old enough to now."

"That's not fair!" Carol said. "You didn't let me sit when I was eleven."

"Janie's proven she can handle herself in an emergency," Mom said.

"I could have handled an emergency, too," Carol said. "I just didn't happen to run into any the way Janie did."

"I'm not really opposed to Janie babysitting," Dad said. "But does she really need the extra work?"

"Not really," I said. I'd been planning on dismantling Kid Power anyway. I'd do those yard sales because they were kind of fun, but I didn't see any reason to take on any new jobs. "I don't mind not doing it."

"Why don't you call that lady back and tell her I'll babysit?" Carol said.

I got mad for a moment, and then decided to calm down. "Sure," I said. "For ten percent."

"Ten percent!" she screeched. "I'll be doing all the work."

"Ten percent," I said. "Those are my final terms. If you don't want it, I'll take the job."

"Daddy?" Carol said, trying to look pathetic.

Dad tried not to smile. "Ten percent seems reasonable to me," he said.

"Fine," I said. "I'll call the lady back right now and tell her what we've decided."

Carol's mouth stayed open while I made the call. I explained that I was booked solid for a while, but that Kid Power would be happy to supply her with another babysitter, my older sister. The lady paused for a moment, and then said common sense usually ran in a family, and if I had it, my sister probably did too, so it was a deal. I hung up and told Carol she had a job for that Friday night. To sweeten her disposition, I also asked her for my standard yard sale order of six dozen oatmeal cookies at our regular rate. I could see Carol computing how much money she'd be earning from me in two days if she stayed on good terms with me, and she smiled to show it was a deal. I smiled, too. It was nice having Carol act nice to me when it wasn't her birthday.

The next morning Mom and I went to the bank to start my account. I had fifty-seven dollars stuffed into my envelope. I'd never seen so much money in my life, let alone had it.

We went to the new-accounts desk and explained the situation. The lady asked me what my name was and I told her.

"You're the girl who rescued Mrs. Edwards!" she exclaimed. "I read about you in the paper yesterday."

I blushed and nodded. Mom grinned.

"Mr. Rivers, come here," the woman said, and a man walked over. "This is Janie Golden, the girl who rescued Mrs. Edwards."

"Ah, yes," he said. "I read about you in the paper yesterday. Congratulations."

"Thank you," I said. I thought my cheeks were on fire.

"Jane wants to start an account with us. From the money she earned from Kid Power, I bet," the woman said.

"I was most impressed with Kid Power," the man said. "So many children start things and then drop them. It sounds like you have a fine organization going."

"It's expanding," I choked out. I hadn't seen Mom smile so much in months.

"We're honored to have your account," the man said. "I hope this is just the start of a long and profitable relationship for both of us."

"Thank you," I said. The man walked away, and the

woman started filling the forms out. Mom and I supplied all the information she needed and signed where we were supposed to. I took the forms to the line and handed them to the teller along with my envelope of money. In return, I got a bank book that listed my savings at fifty-seven dollars. It wasn't a bad start.

Mom decided to treat me to lunch, so we went to a luncheonette and I ordered franks and beans. Mom got a roast beef sandwich. After that we walked around town window-shopping. It had been a long time since we'd done anything together outside the house and we both enjoyed it. I liked knowing that I was earning money without having to do anything, too.

We didn't get home until after two. I found Carol in the kitchen taking a tray of cookies out of the oven.

"I thought you'd never get back," she said. "You've gotten a half-dozen phone calls since you left."

"I did?" I asked, grabbing an apple. "Who from?"

"Lisa called just to say hello," Carol said, wiping her forehead. "So did Ted. Mrs. Edwards called from the hospital to say she got your card and she was feeling much better and she wished she could see you so she could thank you properly. And the other ones are written down on the pad."

I walked over to the pad to check the messages. "Carol, what did you do?" I asked. "These are people who called with jobs for me."

"I said you'd take them," Carol said. "The first one is a lady who needs someone to babysit on Saturday. And one of those people needs someone to help her pack some boxes. I thought that might be an interesting

change of pace. And some lady wants you to walk her Great Dane. I told her animal care was one of your specialties."

"But I can't do all that," I said.

"Why not?" Carol said. "Mom and Dad said you could babysit, so that's no problem."

"You know big dogs scare me," I said, thinking of Sugar. "And I can't pack those boxes. I have a yard sale Saturday. I can't possibly do both."

"I'm sorry," she said. "I just assumed you could."

"Call them back and say you can't make it," Mom said.

"I will," I said, just as the phone rang. I picked it up. "Hello?" I said.

"Is this Kid Power?"

"Yes it is," I said.

"This is Harrison Dowell," the voice said. "I'm calling to confirm that you'll be over on Saturday to help my wife with her yard sale."

I checked my calendar frantically. As far as I could tell, my Saturday yard sale was with a Mrs. Schwartz.

"Your wife didn't call me, did she?" I asked, trying to sound mature.

"No," the man said. "I spoke to your father about it. We take the train together, and I mentioned I'd seen the article about you. Congratulations, by the way."

"Thank you," I said, trying to think fast.

"I thought it would be a pleasant surprise for my wife if you were there to help out. Your father assures me you're quite a competent worker, and I have great faith in your father's judgment."

"Oh," I said. I didn't want to let my father down. Good grief, this was the first I'd heard that he thought I was a competent anything, or that he approved of what I was doing.

"I don't know if I'll be able to be at your yard sale myself," I said. "I have another appointment my father didn't know about."

"Oh," he said. "I'm sorry to hear that."

"But Kid Power represents a number of workers," I said. "I'll supply someone else for the sale if that's all right with you."

I could tell he was thinking. "All right," he said. "Could you have someone over by nine o'clock Saturday morning at 11 Smith Street?"

"I guarantee you'll be satisfied," I said, writing down the information. "Thank you, Mr. Dowell."

"Thank you," he said. "You sound like a very mature young woman."

I didn't want to thank him again, so I just made a mature noise and repeated his address. We said goodbye.

"Carol, can you bake me another batch of cookies?" I asked. "Regular rate?"

"Okay," Carol said. "I guess I owe you that much."

"Thank you," I said.

"What're you going to do now?" she asked, layering the cookies on sheets of wax paper.

"I'm not quite sure," I said. "I think I'm going to try to be an organizational genius."

"Good luck," she said. "You're going to need it." I couldn't even argue.

Chapter Ten

I took all the messages Carol had written down and went up to my room. I took a calendar with me, and a pencil. Then I took a piece of loose-leaf paper and wrote down every job I had scheduled and when I was supposed to do them.

To get everything done I would have needed five extra arms, seven new legs, and a fondness for Great Danes, none of which I had. Of course I could have called half those places back and said I couldn't make it, but that didn't seem right. Dad would be sure to say I'd bitten off more than I could chew if I did, even though he was responsible for part of the mess I was in.

So then I thought about Carol and the babysitting and Lisa and the Townsends' garden and Lisa's mother and the ten percent, and I knew with a little bit of luck I'd be able to get everything done and make some money on it on the side.

First I called Ted, since after all he'd called me. "Hi,

Ted," I said, when he picked up the phone. "How're things going?"

"Okay," he said. "I pitched a no-hitter yesterday and hit three home runs."

"That's pretty good," I said. It had been a long time since I'd played baseball. All work and no play . . . "Say Ted, how would you like to earn a little money?"

"Sure," he said. "I could use a new pitcher's glove."

"You have dogs, don't you?" I asked. I knew he did, but I was favoring the casual approach. Great Danes terrify me, almost as much as German shepherds and scotties.

"Two Saint Bernards," he said. "Waldo and Evangeline."

"I thought so," I said. "You see, this woman called Kid Power and she needs someone to walk her Great Dane. I thought I should give the job to someone with dog experience."

"I thought you did all the jobs in Kid Power," Ted said.

"I'm expanding," I said. "Would you be interested in the job?"

"I guess so," he said. "If I could fit walking the dogs in with my baseball schedule. What's the pay?"

"I'll have to get back to you on that," I admitted. "I take ten percent though."

"That sounds fair," Ted said. "Call me back when you know what's going on, okay?"

"Okay," I said, and hung up. I called the Great Dane lady and explained that I had a young man who was used to big dogs and would therefore be perfect for the job. The woman said that sounded just fine; she had broken her ankle and couldn't walk the dog in the morning, or afternoon. She asked me what the rates were.

I said a dollar for two walks a day, for a five-day week. That meant Ted would be earning $4.50 and I'd be earning fifty cents for doing nothing. It sounded reasonable, and the lady said fine. I promised I'd send Ted right over, so I called him back and told him the terms. He agreed to them and I gave him the woman's name and address. Dog walking now sounded like a good area of expansion for Kid Power.

That took care of the Great Dane, thank goodness. Now all I had to work out were two yard sales, a babysitting job, and box packing all on the same Saturday.

"Carol!" I hollered downstairs.

"What is it?" she hollered back up.

"Are you busy Saturday night?"

"No!"

"Want to babysit?" I asked. "I get ten percent."

"You money-hungry little skinflint!" she called back.

"Ten percent. Take it or leave it."

"I'll take it," she said, so I called the babysitting lady and told her Kid Power Agency would be happy to supply her with a sitter at a dollar an hour. The lady agreed. If Carol sat for four hours, I'd earn forty cents without ever leaving my home. I could understand why Lisa's mother enjoyed being an agent so much.

Of course that still left the problem of having to be three different places at the same time, but I was starting to feel no problem was unconquerable. So I called Margie. Margie's my third best friend. She'd be my second best friend if she didn't talk about kids all the time. She has a real thing for them.

"Hi, Margie," I said. "Do you have anything going on on Saturday?"

"I don't think so," she said. "Why, what's up?"

"Well, I know how good you are with kids," I said. "And I have this job that calls for someone really talented with them."

"For money?" she asked. Margie's a lot shrewder than I think she is sometimes.

"A dollar an hour minus ten percent," I said. "You'll probably make four dollars out of it. Maybe more."

"Doing what?" she asked.

"Looking after kids at a yard sale," I said. "The kind of thing I've been doing."

"Why don't you want the job?"

"Because I already have a yard sale scheduled for myself," I said. "Kid Power's expanding and I need people to help out. Are you willing?"

"Okay," she said. I gave her Mr. Dowell's name and address. "The way I take care of the kids is with oatmeal cookies. I give them away for free," I told her.

"That's a good idea," she said. "I'll bake chocolate chip though. People like chocolate chip cookies more than oatmeal."

I thought of Carol downstairs baking a second batch of oatmeal cookies and how I was going to have to pay for them. But Margie can get really stubborn about things, and besides, I didn't feel like figuring out if she should pay for the cookies or if I should give them to her. So I just said, "That sounds good. It doesn't matter what kind of cookies Kid Power offers, just so long as we have some. It's our trademark."

"Thanks for the job," Margie said. "Taking care of kids is fun. And getting paid for it, too? What a racket!"

The real racket was getting ten percent of whatever she earned, but I didn't tell her that. Instead I hung up with one less problem to solve. Of course, now I had to worry about what to do with all those oatmeal cookies, but I knew if worse came to worse we could eat them as dessert every time we had tuna noodle casserole. At that rate, they'd be gone in no time flat.

I had a couple of choices for box packing. Lisa would be free to help out; Mrs. Townsend's garden didn't take all day, after all. Or Carol might do it. Or even Ted, although it probably would have interfered with his baseball. But I decided to try Sheila first. Kid Power might as well have as many employees as possible. So I dialed the sacred unlisted number and got Sheila on the first ring. It was always a relief when her mother didn't answer the phone, and cross-examine me about how I got the number.

"Hi, Sheila," I said. "You busy on Saturday?"

Sheila wasn't, and packing boxes sounded good to her. So I called the box-packing lady and arranged for Sheila to go over there at one and work until four for a dollar an hour. I did a little mental arithmetic then and decided I'd have to go to the bank on Monday; I'd have earned so much money over the weekend. And earning money felt good to me again.

I made out a chart then, on another piece of loose-leaf paper, with all the days of the week on it and all the jobs I had scheduled and who was going to be doing what. It looked impressive, so I took it downstairs to show Mom and Carol.

They were sitting in the kitchen waiting for the cookies to finish baking. I showed them the piece of paper, and they agreed it looked good. I was just starting to work my nerve up to explain to Carol that her second batch of cookies wasn't necessary after all when the phone rang. I picked it up.

"Hello?" I said.

"Is this Kid Power?" the woman asked.

"Yes it is," I said, almost dreading the thought of another job for the weekend. I'd run out of space on my chart.

"This is Hortense Carson," the woman said. "I purchased your oatmeal cookies at a yard sale."

It was the Oatmeal Cookie Lady! "Yes, I remember you," I said. "What can I do for you?"

"I just found out my church is having a cake sale," Ms. Carson said. "And I hate baking. I was wondering if I could have a rush order on some oatmeal cookies."

"I think we could manage that," I said. "How many cookies would you like?"

"I thought three dozen would be enough," she said. "And another dozen for me if you could. These cookies remind me so much of my childhood."

"Four dozen," I said thoughtfully, looking at all the cookies Carol was taking out of the oven. "I can bring them over right now if you'd like."

"That would be wonderful," she said. "I live at 12 Oakcrest Drive."

"I know where that is," I said. "That's $2.40 for four dozen cookies."

"I know," she said. "It'll certainly be worth that to have homebaked cookies for the sale that I didn't have to bake."

So I agreed to come right over, and bring the cookies with me. I took Carol's first batch, since they were already cool, and I walked over very carefully. Ms. Carson gave me my money, and we thanked each other. It was the easiest $2.40 I ever made, even if $1.50 of it was Carol's.

While I was out, I walked over to the five-and-ten and bought some oak tag and a couple of brand-new magic markers. I took the stuff back with me to my house.

"Hi, Carol," I said, and handed her her $1.50.

"You owe me more than that," she said. "You owe me for all these cookies."

"I do indeed," I said. Luckily, I hadn't deposited all the money I'd earned, so I gave her the rest of the money for the cookies. I had 96 cookies to get rid of on Saturday, but that was a lot better than having 144. That many oatmeal cookies could really make you sick.

"I have another job for you," I said, fingering the oak tag.

"More baking?" she asked. "Forget it."

"Not baking and not babysitting," I said. "Sign making."

"But you already have your sign," she said.

"I need a new one," I said. "I need a lot of new ones and I want you to make them."

"Okay," she said. "For fifty cents a sign."

It was too hot to argue. "Deal," I said. "I need a new one for the supermarket, and one each for the two yard sales. Three altogether."

"What do you want them to say?" she asked, and we walked out to the back porch. There was a slight breeze blowing.

"Kid Power Agency," I said. "I'm bigger than I used to be."

"If you eat all those leftover cookies you'll be a lot bigger," Carol said and giggled. I giggled too. It was a good feeling sitting on the porch getting ready to expand.

"Do you want to keep your slogan?" she asked, nibbling on a slightly burnt cookie. I think she burned a few of them deliberately. "No job too big or small?"

I thought about the Great Dane and Mrs. Townsend's garden and horrible Harriet. "Make that 'Few jobs too big or small,'" I said. "And underneath I want a listing of our specialties."

"Your specialties?" Carol asked. "What? Neurosurgery? Corporation Law?"

"Babysitting," I said. "Animal Care. Gardens."

"Some list," she said.

"Errand Running," I continued. "Yard Sales. And Oatmeal Cookies."

"How about Satisfaction Guaranteed?" she asked. "That always looks good on a sign."

"Fine," I said. "Three signs. One big, two little. The little ones don't have to list our specialties. But make sure our phone number is in big print."

"Will do, Chief," Carol said. I left her on the porch, taking her pencil and sketching in all the information. I was glad I was able to push a little business her way.

I went into the living room and found Mom sitting on the sofa staring at the staircase. I couldn't tell whether that was a good sign or not. At least she wasn't copying recipes. It was spooky when she did that.

"Hi, Mom," I said. "I'm going to make a fortune, and I'm not even going to have to do anything except answer the phone and collect the money."

"You've found quite a racket for yourself," she said. "Now leave me alone, could you hon? I'm doing some serious thinking."

"About what?" I asked nervously.

"About rackets," she said, and smiled. "I think you may have inspired me."

"How?" I asked.

"Shush," she said. "Let me think some more and then I'll tell you."

Chapter Eleven

I may have spent more frantic Saturdays in my life, but I couldn't tell you when.

For starters there was the yard sale I was in charge of. It lasted six hours, and I managed to get rid of most of the oatmeal cookies, at only a small loss to my gross. None of the kids there broke or stole anything, and when the sale was over Mrs. Schwartz gave me a dollar bonus so I stayed a little longer and helped her pack up.

People kept coming up to me and my sign and saying they'd read about me in the paper. They asked a lot of questions about Kid Power Agency and a half-dozen of them took down the name and phone number and said they might have a job coming up for us to do. When I told them about expansion, they agreed that it was a sensible idea. They usually bought a couple of oatmeal cookies after that from the Adult Plate. It was a very profitable afternoon.

I got home by four, absolutely exhausted. Still, I was

glad when Lisa came over. She looked excited about something.

"Mrs. Townsend is back!" she shouted.

I turned pale. "What did she say?" I asked.

"She said the garden looked great. She said she couldn't have tended it better herself."

"Even with the Japanese beetles?" I asked dubiously.

"Especially with the beetles," Lisa said. "Mrs. Townsend said they've been eating away at her garden for the past couple of years, and she never did know what to do about them. She was really happy when I told her my method."

"What exactly is your method?" I asked. I'd been wondering about it.

"I read about it in a magazine," Lisa said and giggled. "You take an open can of fruit cocktail, and you leave it outside for a week, so it ferments a little. Then you put it in a bucket of water and leave it by the rosebushes. The Japanese beetles eat the fruit cocktail and get drunk and drown in the water. Isn't that great?"

"That's horrible," I said and giggled, too. "I just wish I'd known about that method earlier."

"For Mrs. Townsend's garden?" Lisa asked.

"What, Mrs. Townsend's garden," I said. "For Harriet!"

"You're terrible," Lisa said, and joined me laughing. "Anyway, Mrs. Townsend was so happy with the job we did, she gave me a five dollar bonus."

A person could sure grow attached to those bonuses. "Keep it," I said. "You're the one who deserves it."

"I thought we'd split it," she said firmly. "You did

most of the work and all of the worrying. You deserve at least half."

It was hard to argue with that logic. So I added another $2.50 profit to my day's accounts.

"Not only that," Lisa said. "But when Mrs. Townsend was in the hospital she heard about Mrs. Edwards, and she said she thought that was a great idea, having someone come in every day to check up on her and see if she needs anything. So I'm going to go over for fifty cents a day. Minus ten percent of course."

"That's great," I said, sinking into an easy chair. "Lisa, if any more garden jobs come up, you want them?"

"I'd love them," Lisa said. "I like making money."

"It is fun," I said.

We heard shouting outside, then, so we went out front to see what was going on. It was Ted, calling to us. He was walking the biggest Great Dane I'd ever seen. I stayed behind Lisa as we walked over to say hello.

"This is a great job," Ted said. "I wasn't supposed to walk this dog on weekends, but they decided to go away for the afternoon and I offered to take care of him. The more I walk him, the sooner I get my new glove."

"Don't forget my ten percent," I said.

"I'll pay you on Monday," he said. "Monday's our payment day."

"Fine," I said, as the dog dragged Ted away.

And then Margie came. She looked as tired as me.

"All those kids," she said, and smiled happily. "Thousands of them. And they all loved my chocolate chip cookies. Except for a couple who said the yard sale down the street had better oatmeal ones."

"They're Carol's specialty," I said.

"I owe you sixty cents," she said, handing me a dollar. So I gave her forty cents change. Earning money really seemed easy when you had other people doing it for you.

The three of us talked for a while, mostly about our different jobs, and what we'd be willing to do if Kid Power Agency got any more assignments. Margie said a lot of people took down the phone number from her sign. We all agreed we were on to a good thing, at least for the rest of the summer. When school started, we'd cut down on our jobs.

The phone rang, and Carol stuck her head out to say it was for me. So I ran into the kitchen, and everybody left for their houses.

"Is this Kid Power?" a woman asked irritably.

"Yes it is," I said, and grabbed a paper and pencil.

"This is Mrs. Schuman," the woman said. "You were supposed to send someone over to help me pack boxes. Three hours, three dollars."

"That's right," I said. "Didn't the girl I sent show up?"

"Nobody has," Mrs. Schuman said. "I read about you in the paper, and it said how responsible you were, but I must say I'm deeply disappointed. I'm moving tomorrow you know."

"I'll have someone over in half an hour," I promised. "Fifteen minutes. I promise."

"Well," she said.

"And if you don't like the service, you don't have to pay," I said. "Fifteen minutes."

"All right then," she said, and we hung up. I felt like killing Sheila. Instead I dialed her number. After two rings, an operator's voice came on and said the phone had been disconnected.

That could only mean Sheila's mother was having one of her crises, which would explain why Sheila hadn't shown up. But it also meant there was no way of getting through to her.

"Carol!" I shouted.

"What?" she asked, coming into the kitchen.

"Want another job?" I asked. "Please, it's an emergency."

"When?" she asked.

"Right now," I said.

"I can't," she said. "I promised Gwen I'd go over to her house before supper."

I was going to say something about what was more important, but then I remembered Lisa and how mad she'd been at me. "What am I going to do?" I said instead. "It's too late for me to try to get anybody else."

"Then you'll have to do it yourself," Carol said. "It's called responsibility."

"I'm learning," I said, and grabbed the piece of paper with Mrs. Schuman's address on it. "Tell Mom and Dad I'll be home late for supper. But before dark. And tell Dad it'll never happen again."

"Good luck," Carol said.

I ran all the way to Mrs. Schuman's. Maybe it was the way I was panting when I introduced myself, or maybe it was the way I did nothing but apologize for the first five minutes, but Mrs. Schuman turned out not to be a grouch. She did expect a lot of hard work though, packing things and moving the boxes. My muscles really ached from the yard sale before I got there. After three hours of practically nonstop work, I was ready to find a nursing home and retire for good.

"Well," Mrs. Schuman said at seven-thirty. "I'd say we got a lot accomplished."

We sure had. There were more boxes loaded and labeled than I'd ever seen in my life. "You don't have to pay me," I said, although I think I would have cried if she hadn't. My body never hurt so much in my life.

"You've earned your pay," she said, and handed me three dollars. "I admire the job you're doing. Keep up the good work."

"Thank you," I said. "Good luck on your move."

"It's going to be a lot easier now," she said, and we said good-bye. I walked slowly all the way home. I wasn't looking forward to what Dad was going to say about the hours I had to put in, but all he did when I got in was give me a hug and say, "We all have rough days occasionally."

Mom had made a huge chef's salad for supper, and for dessert I'd contributed a few spare oatmeal cookies. We were sitting at the dinner table feeling relaxed and happy. Carol had to leave in a little bit for her babysitting job, but making extra money always puts her in a good mood, so we were all feeling fine.

"I have an idea," Mom said, sipping her iced tea. "Something to keep me busy until I find a job."

"That sounds good," Dad said. He didn't say anything about sore feet or tuna casseroles or copying recipes. I breathed a sigh of relief.

"Kid Power is such a success," she said. "I thought it might not hurt to try an adult version."

"What do you mean?" I asked.

"A lot of housewives would like part-time occasional jobs to help pick up a little extra money," Mom said. "And I think this summer's proved there are a lot of occasional jobs out there needing to be filled. So I thought maybe I'd try to organize something to take care of both needs."

"What kind of jobs?" I asked. I didn't like the idea of Mom directly competing with me.

"Adult kinds of jobs," she said, answering my unasked question. "Cooking for invalids. Gourmet cooking. Helping with parties. Chauffeuring. Daytime babysitting. I'm sure there are a dozen more things if I thought about it."

"It certainly sounds like it's worth a try," Dad said. "Although we may have to get the two of you a new phone number."

"Well, let's not rush out and order one," Mom said. "I thought I'd take August and investigate possibilities. And then once I got things organized I'd sit back and collect my ten percent. Just like Janie."

"It sure is fun," I said, thinking about Carol and Lisa and Ted and Margie. "Doing nothing and getting paid for it."

"You don't do nothing," Mom said. "You assign the jobs, and make sure the people are doing them and doing them well."

It hadn't occurred to me before, but after Mrs. Schuman, I'd learned my lesson. So I nodded. "Like tonight," I said. "I'll make sure Carol does okay at her babysitting. I wouldn't want one bad apple to ruin Kid Power Agency."

"Good grief," Carol muttered, but then she smiled at me. Even taking out ten percent from her pay, she was still making fifteen cents more an hour for the Kid Power babysitting jobs than she'd ever gotten on her own. I didn't know how long it would last, but for the time being, I knew she'd be fairly friendly.

"Good lord," Dad said, staring at me like he'd never seen me before. "What a calling."

"What do you mean?" I asked.

"Everybody has a true calling," he said. "Some people find it later than others though. You're the first eleven-year-old I've ever met who knows hers."

"What's mine?" I asked. I could think of quite a few things it wasn't. Gardening, for one, or modeling, and it certainly wasn't walking German shepherds.

"Management," Dad said and scowled. "Here I am a labor lawyer, and for my daughter I have an eleven-year-old management whiz. An exploiter of the working class, all for her ten percent. It's disgraceful."

"Don't worry, Dad," Carol said. "I'll unionize."

"No picket lines, please," Mom said. "At least not on our front lawn."

But I didn't care about Carol and her threats. I was feeling too good. Picket lines or no, management sounded like a pretty good true calling to me.

About the Author

Susan Beth Pfeffer has always been an author. She grew up in New York, was graduated from New York University, and now lives in Middletown, New York. She is the author of more than ten novels, and her stories and articles have appeared in *American Girl*, *Young Miss*, and *Ellery Queen Mystery Magazine*.

The idea for this story began one day when she was feeling very poor, and it came out as pure wish fulfillment.